INVASION

Having just about concluded that it was nothing more than the wind and the storm that was upsetting the horses — and now they were all leaping and snorting more furiously than ever, as if they were not three ordinary nags but a trio of high-strung thoroughbreds — I turned toward the door and quite accidentally caught sight of the light which glowed eerily just beyond the only window in the entire building. There were two lights, actually, both a warm amber shade and of dim wattage. They appeared to pulse and to shimmer — and then they were gone, as if they had never been: blink!

I hurried to the barn door, slid it open, and stepped into the snow-filled night. The arctic wind struck me like a mallet swung by a blacksmith who was angry with his wife, and it almost blew me back into the stable row. Switching on the nearly useless flashlight, I bent against the wind and pulled the door shut behind me. Laboriously, cautiously, I inched around the side of the barn in the direction of the window, peering anxiously at the ground ahead of me.

I stopped before I reached the window, for I found precisely what I had been afraid that I would find: those odd, eight-pointed tracks which Toby and I had seen on the slope earlier in the day. There were a great many of them, as if the animal had been standing there, moving back and forth as it searched for better vantage points, for a long while — at least all of the time that I had been inside with the horses.

It had been watching me.

THE FIRST TWELVE
LASER BOOKS

AARON WOLFE

INVASION

COVER
ILLUSTRATION
BY
KELLY
FREAS

INVASION

A LASER BOOK/first published 1975

Copyright © 1975 by Aaron Wolfe

ISBN 0-373-72009-2

Printed in U.S.A.

INTRODUCTION
by
Barry Malzberg

The world is a madhouse.
Death is real and final.
Somewhere between these two poles where the narrative of Aaron Wolfe's novel occurs something else happens: it becomes a vision.

This is Aaron Wolfe's first novel. Thirty-four years old and successful in another artistic field he has asked for compelling personal reasons that his real identity not interfere with his fiction and therefore "Aaron Wolfe" is a pseudonym. He is thirty-four years old, married with one child and lives in the midwestern United States.

Aaron Wolfe's work has appeared in *Escapade, Alfred Hitchcock's Mystery Magazine* and the *Virginia Quarterly*; fiction and poetry. He was the recipient of a North American Review writing fellowship in 1965 and one of his stories published that year appeared on the Martha Foley Roll of Honor of distinguished American short stories. INVASION, nonetheless, is his first novel and his first work of science-fiction.

"I've always loved to read science-fiction," he says, confessing to owning a "large collection" of old pulp magazines and anthologies, "and even have a passion for it. I've been addicted since I was ten and when I sit down with a science-fiction novel I'm like a child again. Who could react otherwise to this marvelous stuff?"

INVASION gives some indication of what a literary writer of the first rank can do when he essays fiction for a wider audience. It is simply one of the most remarkable first novels, in any field, that I have ever read.

Other comments relevant to my role in the Laser Book series, how it came about and what I take my own role to be may be found in my introduction to K. W. Jeter's SEEKLIGHT, the first of this group of novels published recently, and I refer the reader, gratefully, to that.

Barry Malzberg
New Jersey.

WEDNESDAY

The Beginning

1.

The three-hundred-acre Timberlake Farm, which we were renting that year, was as isolated a refuge as you could possibly find in New England. Elsewhere highways had cut open regions once closed to man by dense pine forests and rocky landscapes; and the small towns, previously content with their unsophisticated ways, had begun to build industrial "parks" to lure manufacturers from the choked cities; and the suburbs continued to sprawl, gobbling up the open countryside, macadamizing and concretizing and tract-housing the woodlands. Contemptuous of the noise and the grime of civilization, northern Maine shunned highways that went nowhere; and it did not welcome commuters who wanted to move into the snow country with their big cars and snowmobiles and aluminum-redwood houses. Some day, of course, when the population pressure reached an unbearable peak, even Timberlake Farm would be filled with lookalike, two-bedroom ranch houses and condominium apartment buildings; however, the year that we lived there the farmhouse was two miles from the nearest neighbor and eleven miles from the nearest town, Barley, Maine.

Isolated.

Perhaps *too* isolated.

But that realization was not to come to us until December, after we had lived on the farm for more than six months. And then it was definitely too late for second thoughts.

The farmhouse was a two-story flagstone manor with four large bedrooms, three baths, a drawing room, study, pine-panelled library, formal dining room, and modern kitchen. The luxury was greater than one might expect to find in a farmhouse in Maine—but Timberlake had been conceived as a gentleman's retreat and not as an enterprise that must support itself. The land had never been cultivated, and the barn had never contained any animals but riding horses.

Isolation:

The house had one telephone, the lines for which had been run in at no little expense by Creighton Development, the company that owned and rented the property through Blackstone Realty in Barley. It was completely furnished except for a television set—and we had early decided to do without *that* questionable luxury in favor of books and conversation.

Isolation:

Every two weeks the three of us drove in to Barley in our Volkswagen microbus. We might take in a movie at the Victory Theater, and we always had dinner at the Square Restaurant. We picked up new magazines and paperbacks at the cigar store across the street from the restaurant. That was the full extent—aside from rare telephone calls and the occasional letter we received in the weekly maildrop at the end of our lane—of our contact with the outside world.

Initially, that was all we required. But once the snows came and the trouble began, we damned our isolation a hundred times a day and wished fervently for contact with people outside our family, with anyone at all. . .

The first major blizzard of the year began on the twelfth day of December, late in the afternoon, when there was already eight inches of early-season snow on the ground. Toby and I were in the woods to the north of the house, tracking the foxes, snow rabbits, weasels, squirrels, and the few cats that kept active until the snow was so deep, even under the trees, that they were forced to remain in their caves, burrows, and nests. Toby's favorite pastime was tracking and spying upon our animal neighbors. I enjoyed the gentle sport as much as he did—perhaps because it *was* gentle, perhaps because I was proud that my son had never once suggested that we go up to the house and get a rifle and hunt down the animals. We were deep in the forest that afternoon, hot on the trail of a fox, when the snow began to sift heavily between the pine boughs, so heavily that we knew a bad storm must be sweeping across the open land, beyond the shelter of the woods. By the time we had followed our own trail back to the edge of the woods, a new inch of snow lay atop the old eight inches; and the farmhouse at the top of the rise three hundred yards away was all but invisible behind shifting curtains of flakes.

"Will it be deep?" Toby asked.

"I'm afraid so," I said.

"I like it deep."

"You would."

"Real deep."

"It'll be over your head," I told him. For a ten-year-old boy he was somewhat slender and a bit short; therefore, I wasn't exaggerating all that much when I held my hand over his head so that he could look up and see how far it would be to the surface if he should become buried in new snow.

"Great!" he said, as if the notion of being buried alive in a drift were too close to paradise to be borne. He ran off to the right and scooped up a handful of new snow and threw it at me. But it was too dry to pack into a ball, and it only flew apart and blew back on him when he tossed it.

"Come on, Toby. We better get back to the house before we're stranded down here." I held out my hand to him, hoping that he would take it. Ten-year-old boys usually insist on proving their self-reliance; but thirty-year-old fathers would much rather have them dependent, just a little bit, just for a few more years, just enough to need a hand to negotiate a slippery hillside.

He grinned broadly and started back towards me —then stopped a dozen feet away and stared at the ground. From the way he was bent over, and from the intensity of his gaze, I knew that he had come across a set of tracks and was puzzling out the nature of the animal that had made them.

We had been tramping through the forest for more than three hours, and I was ready for a warm fireplace and a vodka martini and a pair of felt-lined slippers. The wind was sharp; snowflakes found their way under my coat collar and down by back. "There'll be hot chocolate up at the house," I told him.

He didn't say anything or look up at me.

"And a plate of doughnuts."

He said nothing.

"Doughnuts, Toby."

"This is something new," he said, pointing to the tracks in front of him.

"Marshmallows for the hot chocolate," I said, even though I knew I was losing the battle. No adult can achieve the single-minded determination of a child.

"Look at this, Dad."

"A game of Monopoly while we eat. How about that?"

"Dad, look at this," he insisted.

So I went and looked.

"What is it?"

I went around behind him in order to see the tracks from his vantage point.

He frowned and said, "It's not a fox or a weasel or a squirrel. That's for sure. I can spot one of those right away. It kind of looks like the mark a bird would leave, huh Dad? A bird's tracks—but funny."

These marks certainly were "funny." As I took in the pattern of a single print, I felt the skin on the back of my neck tremble, and the air seemed to be a bit colder than it had been only a moment ago. The print consisted of eight separate indentations. There were three evenly spaced holes in the snow —each of them four inches in front of the other— parallel to a second set of holes two feet to the right of the first line. The marks were all identical, as if they had been stamped in the snow by a man's walking cane. Equidistant from both sets of holes and better than a yard in front of them, there was a pair of similar indentations, although each of these was as large across as the bottom of a standard water glass. It looked like this:

Although I was rather well acquainted with the woods, I had never seen anything remotely like it before. If all of that were indeed a single print, the animal was quite large, certainly not a bird of any kind.

"What is it, Dad?" Toby asked. He squinted up at me, his eyelashes frosted with snowflakes, his nose like a berry, the bill of his red cap fringed with ice. He was certain that I would have the answer.

I said, "I don't really know."

For an instant his disappointment in me was all too evident—then he quickly covered his feelings, changed his expression, broke into a tentative smile. That made me sad, for it was an indication that he understood Dad was still on shaky psychological ground and needed all the love and affection he could get. Otherwise, Dad might end up in the hospital again, staring at the walls and not talking and not at all like Dad should be.

"Can we follow it?" Toby asked.

"We ought to be getting home."

"Ahh, heck."

"Your nose is as red as a stoplight."

"I'm tough," he said.

"I know you are. I wouldn't argue about that. But your mother is expecting us about now." I pointed to the rapidly vanishing set of prints. "Besides, the wind and snow will have these filled in within a few minutes. We couldn't track them very far."

He glanced back toward the trees, squinted his

eyes as if he were trying to dispel the shadows under the pine boughs. "Then, whatever it was, it went by here just before we came out of the woods, huh Dad?"

That was true enough, although I hadn't thought about it. "When the storm's finished, maybe we can come out and look for new tracks," I said.

"On snowshoes?"

"Have to use snowshoes if the snow's over your head."

"Great!" he said, dismissing the mystery that suddenly. If we could all remain small boys in at least one tiny corner of our minds, we would never end up in private, locked rooms in silent hospitals, staring at walls and refusing to speak. . .

"At least we can follow this trail until it turns away from the house," I said.

He gave me his hand, and we bent our heads against the wind, keeping a close watch on the odd prints as we climbed the slope. The holes were repeated in exactly the same pattern until we were halfway up the hill to the house. At the mid-point of the slope, the prints stopped in a much trampled circle of snow. Toby found the place where they struck off once again toward another arm of the pine forest.

"It stood here," Toby said. "It stood right here and watched our house for a long time."

Indeed, the animal, whatever it might be, seemed to have come out of the woods solely to stare at the farmhouse and, once its curiosity was satisfied, had gone away again. But I didn't like to think that was the case. There was some indefinable alien quality about those prints—which were so unlike anything I had ever before encountered—that made me at first

15

uneasy and eventually somewhat frightened. That fear, as irrational as it might have been, only increased when I contemplated the thing standing here on this windblown slope, watching the farmhouse where Connie had spent the entire afternoon alone.

But that was ridiculous.

Wasn't it?

Yes.

What was there to fear?

It was only an animal.

I was being childish.

"Maybe it was a bear," Toby said.

"No. A bear's paws wouldn't leave a trail like this."

"I can't wait to go looking for it on snowshoes."

Well, that's for another day," I said. "Come on."

He wanted to look at the prints some more.

I kept hold of his hand and started toward the house again, setting a faster pace than we'd been keeping. "Remember that hot chocolate!" But I wasn't thinking about hot chocolate at all.

2.

By the time we reached the sun porch at the rear of the house, the wind had the fury of a bomb blast. It followed us through the door, driving a cloud of snow onto the porch.

We did the traditional things people do when they come in from a cold day: we stamped our feet, slapped our arms against our sides, *whooshed!* out our breath, and commented on the clouds of steam. By the time we had stripped off our coats, gloves, and boots, Connie really did have cocoa ready for us in the kitchen.

"Great!" Toby said, climbing onto his chair and poking at the half-dissolved marshmallows with his spoon.

"Don't you know any other expletive besides 'Great'?" I asked.

"Expliv-what?" he asked.

"What you say when you're excited. When something really strikes you as good and wonderful, don't you have anything to say except *great*?"

He frowned into his chocolate, thinking about it for a second or two. Then: "Fabulous!"

"Well, it offers variety," I said.

Fifteen minutes later, fatigued by his long afternoon of stalking the native fauna, Toby nearly fell asleep in his mug of cocoa.

"I'll have to take the scout to bed for a nap," Connie said. She was smiling at him, and she was very pretty.

"I'll do it," I said.

"Sure?"

"Sure," I said. "I'd appreciate having something a bit stronger than hot chocolate once I get him tucked in. Do you think that could be arranged?"

"Possibly."

"Vodka martinis?"

"Just the right medicine for a cold day."

"Especially in large doses."

"I'll mix a pitcherful. I need some medicine myself."

"You were in a toasty warm house all afternoon."

She smiled. "Ah, but I empathize with your frostbite so well. I can *feel* how chilled you are."

"I think you're just a lush."

"That too."

I lifted Toby in my arms and carried him upstairs to his bedroom at the far end of the main hall. He was not much help undressing himself, for he kept nodding off. I finally got him under the covers and pulled the blankets up to his chin. In seconds his eyelids fluttered shut, and he was sound asleep.

The storm sky was so dark that there was no need for me to draw the drapes at the two large, mullioned windows. The wind moaned softly against the glass: an eerie but effective lullaby.

For a while I stood and watched him, and I thought how he would be after his nap: bouncy, energetic, full of ideas and projects and games. When he woke, he would be fascinated by the accumulation of new snow, as if he had not known a storm was in progress when he went to bed. Before we could eat dinner, we would have to step outside in our boots and measure the snow with a yardstick. And that would bring full circle one of the routines that I enjoyed so much: put him to bed, wake him, take him out to marvel at the snow. In the summer, there had been other routines, but they had been just as good as this one.

Downstairs, Connie was sitting by the fireplace where she had put a match to some well-dried birch logs. The sight of her warmed me as the fire could never do. She was a slender but shapely blonde who had celebrated her thirtieth birthday the week before but who might have passed for a teenager without makeup. She was not really beautiful in any conventional sense. She did not resemble a fashion model or a movie star. She had too many freckles for that. Her mouth was much too wide and her nose a little too long for classic beauty. Yet every feature was in harmony with every other feature in her gentle face. and the overall effect was immensely sensuous and appealing. Her best feature was her eyes which were enormous, round, and blue. They were the wide-open, innocent, curious eyes of a fawn. She always looked as if she had just been startled; she was not capable of that sultry, heavy-eyed look that most men found sexy. But that was fine with me. Her beauty was all the better because it was unique and approachable.

I sat down on the couch beside her, put my arm around her, and accepted the drink she had poured for me. It was cold, bitter, very refreshing.

"That's some son you've raised," I said.

"You've raised him too."

"I don't take credit where it isn't due," I said.

19

After all, I had been in the army for two years, eighteen long months in Southeast Asia. And after that, for more than two years, there had been that gray-walled hospital room where Toby had been allowed to visit only twice, and after *that* I'd spent another eight months in a private sanitarium. . .

"Don't be so hard on yourself," she said. She leaned her head against my shoulder. Her pale hair spilled like a fan of golden feathers across my chest. I could feel the pulse throbbing in her temple.

We stayed like that for a while: working at our drinks and watching the fire and not saying anything at all. When I first got out of the hospital, we didn't talk much because neither of us knew quite what to say. I felt terribly guilty about having withdrawn from them and from my responsibilities to them that I was embarrassed about suddenly moving in as an equal member of the family. She hadn't known what to say, for she had been desperately afraid of saying something, anything, that might send me back into my quasicatatonic trance. Hesitantly, fumblingly, we had eventually found our way back to each other. And then there was a time when we could say whatever we chose, a time in which we talked too much and made up for lost years—or perhaps we were afraid that if we didn't say it all now, share it now, immediately, we would have no chance to say it in the future. In the last two months we had settled into a third stage in which we were again sure of each other, as we had been before I went away to war and came back not myself. We didn't feel, as we had, that it was necessary for us to jabber at each other in order to stave off the silences. We were comfortable with long pauses, reveries. . . So: the fire, the drinks, her hair, her quick heartbeat, her hand curling in mine.

And then for no apparent reason—except, perhaps, that it was all too good; I was still frightened of things being too good and therefore having nowhere to go but down again—I thought of the odd tracks in the snow. I told her about them, but with detachment, as if I were talking about something I had read in a magazine.

She said, "What do you think made them?"

"I haven't any idea."

"Maybe you could find it in one of those books in the den. A drawing or photograph just like what you saw."

"I hadn't thought of that," I said. "I'll check it out after dinner." The den was furnished with a shelf of books on woodlore, hunting, rifle care and other "manly" subjects in addition to its studded leather furniture.

"Whatever it is—could it be dangerous?"

"No, no."

"I don't mean dangerous for us—but maybe for a little guy like Toby."

"I don't think so," I said. "It didn't seem to have claws—though it must be fairly large. Toby mentioned a bird. I can't imagine what kind of bird, but I guess it might be that."

"The largest birds around here are pheasants," she said. "And those tracks sound too big for pheasants."

"Much too big," I said.

"Maybe we shouldn't let Toby go outside by himself until we know what we've got on our hands."

I finished my drink and put the glass on the coffee table. "Well, if the books don't give me a clue, I'll call Sam Caldwell and see if he can put me on the right track. If Sam's never seen anything like them, then they're just figments of our imaginations."

Sam was seventy years old, but he still operated his sporting goods store on the square in Barley. He hunted and fished through every legal season, for every breed of creature natural to New England. The way his face was weathered—cut across with a hundred lines and deeply tanned by sun and wind— he even *looked* like a piece of the forest.

As happened often lately, our admiration for the crackling fire swiftly metamorphosed into admiration for each other, and we began some playful necking. The playfulness gave way to real interest: the kisses grew longer, the embraces firmer. Certain that Toby would be asleep for another hour or so, I had just begun to get really serious with her when she drew back a bit and cocked her head, listening.

I said, "What is it?"

"*Ssshh!*"

When my heartbeat subsided and my breathing was somewhat less stentorian than it had been, I could hear it too: the whinnying cries of the horses "Just the nags."

"I wonder what's wrong with them?"

"They know that we're sitting in here getting lovey, and they're jealous. That's all it is. They think we ought to be out there grooming them."

"I'm serious."

I sighed. "Horses sometimes get spooked for no good reason at all." I tried to embrace her again.

She was still intent upon listening to the horses, and she shushed me and held me off.

I said, "I know I locked the barn doors—so it can't be that the wind is bothering them."

"What about the heaters?"

"They've been switched on since the last week of October," I said. "I never touch them."

"You're certain?"

"Of course."

"Well. . . Maybe the heaters have broken down, and the barn's gotten cold."

Reluctantly I let go of her and leaned away from her. "You want me to see about it?"

"Would you?"

"Right away," I said, punctuating it with a well delivered sigh of regret.

"I'm sorry, Don," she said, her gazelle eyes wide and blue and absolutely stunning. "But I can't be happy. . . I can't feel romantic if those poor horses are out there freezing."

I got up. "Neither can I," I admitted. Their squeals were really pitiful. "Though I'd have given it a good try."

"I'll get your coat."

"And my scarf and gloves and stocking cap and frostbite medicine," I said.

She gave me one last smile to keep me warm in the snowstorm. It wasn't the sort of smile most men got from their wives: it was much too seductive for that, too smoky and sultry, not in the least bit domestic.

Five minutes later she huddled in the unheated, glass-enclosed sun porch while I pulled on my boots and zipped them up. As I was about to leave she grabbed me by one arm and pulled me down and gave me a quick kiss on the cheek.

"When I come back from psychoanalyzing the horses," I warned her, "I'm going to chase you around and around the living room sofa until I catch you."

"In a fair race you won't catch me."

"Then I'll cheat."

"Toby will be waking up in half an hour or so," she said, using one slender hand to push her blond hair behind her right ear. "I'm afraid we've lost the opportunity."

"Oh yeah?"

She gave me a saucy look. "Yeah."

"Well, it's about time that kid learned the facts of life anyway, don't you think?"

"Not by watching Daddy chase Mommy around the sofa," she said.

"Then I'll tell you what."

She grinned. "What?"

"While I'm out in the barn clubbing the horses unconscious so they can't interrupt us again, why don't you tie Toby in bed? Then, even if he woke up he couldn't interfere with us."

"How clever."

"Aren't I?"

She shook her head in mock exasperation, gave me another of those dazzling smiles, and pushed me through the sun porch door and into the blinding snowfall.

3.

Darkness came early at that time of year, and the dense snow clouds had ushered it in half an hour ahead of schedule. I switched on the flashlight that I had brought with me—and mumbled some very nasty things about the manufacturer who had foisted it upon an unsuspecting public. It cut through the darkness and a thick rush of snowflakes for all of two or three feet—which was like trying to put out a raging bonfire with a child's toy water pistol. Indeed, the sight of all those wildly jiggling and twisting snowflakes in the wan orange shaft of light made me so dizzy that I turned off the torch and made my way to the barn by sheer instinct; however, since the barn was only two hundred feet from the house, the journey was hardly one that would unduly strain my sense of direction, meager as it was.

Born and raised in upstate New York, I had seen my share of major winter storms, but I had never seen anything to compare with this one. The wind had to be cutting up the curve of the hill at more than forty miles an hour. There was a wicked edge to it like the frayed tip of a bullwhip tearing at bare skin; and it produced a chill factor that must have lowered the temperature to a subjective twenty degrees below zero, or worse. It felt like worse. The snow was falling so heavily now that it appeared to be a horizontal avalanche moving from west to east across the Maine countryside. Already, four inches of the dry, grainy pellets had piled up over the path that I had shoveled along the brow of the hill after the previous snow—and there was considerably more than four inches in those places where the wind had built drifts against some obstacle or other.

And the noise! In sequin-dotted Christmas card art and in quaint landscape paintings, snow scenes always look so pleasant, quiet and gentle and peaceful, a good place to curl up and go to sleep. In reality the worst storms are howling, shrieking beasts that can out-decibel any summer thunder shower in a contest of voices. Even with the flaps of my hat pulled down over my ears, I could hear the horrible keening and moaning of the wind. By the time I was twenty steps from the sun porch door, I had a nagging headache.

Snowflakes swept up my nostrils.

Snowflakes trickled down under my collar.

The wind tore tears from my eyes.

I needed four times as long as usual to reach the barn doors, and I stumbled into them with some shouting and much pain before I realized I had come that far. I fumbled at the lock and slid the bolt back, even though my fingers were so cold that they did not want to curl around the wrought-iron pull. Quickened by the elements, I stepped inside and slammed the door behind me, relieved to be out of the whip of the wind and away from those choruses of banshees that had been intent on blowing out both of my eardrums.

In the warm barn the snow on my eyebrows melted instantly and seeped down my face.

In the truest and strictest sense of the word, the building was not really a barn, for it lacked a loft and animal pens and the traditional machinery found in a barn. Only one story high, it ran straight along the crest of the hill: ten spacious horse stalls on the left and seven on the right, storage bins for grain and meal at the end of the right-hand side, saddles stored on the sawhorses in the corner, grooming instruments and blankets and water buckets racked on the wall just above the saddles.

Many years ago, if the people down at Blackstone Realty were to be believed, some wealthy gentleman farmer had bred several race horses here, mostly for his own amusement; now, however, there were only two sorry mares named Kate and Betty, both of them fat and accustomed to luxuries that they had never earned—plus a pony for Toby, name of Blueberry. All three of the animals were extremely agitated, rolling their eyes and snorting. They kicked at the back walls of their stalls. They slammed their shoulders into the wooden partitions that separated them. They raised their long and elegant necks and cried out, their black nostrils flaring and their brown eyes wide with terror.

"Whoa now, whoa now," I said gently, quietly, trying my best to reassure them. "Calm yourselves, ladies. Everything's all right. Whoa down now. Just you whoa down."

I couldn't see what had them so disturbed. The heating units were all functioning properly. The air in the barn was circulating at a pleasant sixty-nine degrees. I walked the length of the place and looked into the empty stalls. But no stray dog or fox had gotten in through some undiscovered chink in the clapboard walls; the horses were alone.

27

When I tried to calm Blueberry, she snapped at me and just missed taking a sizeable chunk out of my right hand. I had never seen her behave like this before. She peeled her black lips back from her teeth as if she thought she were a guard dog instead of a horse. We had bought her for Toby because she was so gentle and manageable. What had happened, what had changed her temperament so radically and so quickly?

"Whoa now. Whoa girl."

But she simply wasn't going to calm down. She snorted and whinnied and kicked at the back wall of her stall, kicked so hard that a board splintered with a crisp, dry sound.

Oddly enough Kate and Betty were more amenable than Blueberry, even though they both had slight mean streaks. They stopped crying out and ceased kicking their stalls apart as I stroked their faces and rubbed behind their ears. But even they would not come completely under control. They whuffled like dogs and rolled their eyes from side to side.

I remembered that horses are especially sensitive to fire: the odor of sparking wood, the distant crackle of the first flames, the initial traces of smoke . . . Though I sniffed like a bloodhound, I could not sense anything but hay, straw, dust, sweat, and the peculiarly mellow odor of well-used leather saddles and reins. I examined the small oil-fed furnace that warmed the stable. I felt the wall around the fuel tank. I studied the heaters a second time. But I could not find any sign of danger or any malfunction.

Yet Blueberry reared up and whinnied.

And the other two were becoming agitated once more.

Having just about concluded that it was nothing

28

more than the wind and the storm that was upsetting them—and now they were all leaping and snorting more furiously than ever, as if they were not three ordinary nags but a trio of high-strung thoroughbreds —I turned toward the door and quite accidentally caught sight of the light which glowed eerily just beyond the only window in the entire building. There were two lights, actually, both a warm amber shade and of dim wattage. They appeared to pulse and to shimmer—and then they were gone, as if they had never been: *blink!*

I hurried to the barn door, slid it open, and stepped into the snow-filled night. The arctic wind struck me like a mallet swung by a blacksmith who was angry with his wife, and it almost blew me back into the stable row. Switching on the nearly useless flashlight, I bent against the wind and pulled the door shut behind me. Laboriously, cautiously, I inched around the side of the barn in the direction of the window, peering anxiously at the ground ahead of me.

I stopped before I reached the window, for I found precisely what I had been afraid that I would find: those odd, eight-pointed tracks which Toby and I had seen on the slope earlier in the day. There were a great many of them, as if the animal had been standing there, moving back and forth as it searched for better vantage points, for a long while—at least all of the time that I had been inside with the horses.

It had been watching me.

Suddenly I felt as if I were back in Southeast Asia —in a jungle rather than in a snowstorm—where an enemy was relentlessly stalking me.

Ridiculous, of course.

It was only some animal.

A dumb animal.

I swept the flashlight beam around the hilltop and found where the prints continued a few feet away. Though I didn't want to use the flashlight and alert my prey, I couldn't follow the trail without it. The December night was perfectly black and empty once you got away from the light that spilled from the house and from the single stable window. Holding the flashlight before me as if it were a sword, I walked westward, after the animal.

Wind.

Snow.

More wind.

More snow.

Two minutes later I had lost the trail. The wind and snow had conspired to blot out the prints, scouring the land as clean and smooth as a new cotton sheet.

Yet that didn't seem possible. Certainly, the snow was falling very hard and fast. Equally as certain: the wind was ugly. But the creature could have had no more than a two-minute head start on me. The storm couldn't have erased every trace of it so quickly. Unless . . . Unless it was not moving away from me at the same ponderous pace at which *I* moved. If, in the instant that it turned away from the stable window, it had run, and if it could run incredibly fast in spite of the bad weather, it might have gotten a five-minute head start and its tracks might easily have filled up and it might be a mile away by now.

But what sort of animal could move so easily and surely in wind like this, on a night when visibility was near zero?

Considering that, I had to consider one other thing which I had not wanted to think about just yet. I had seen two amber lights at the window, low lights

30

very much like candle flames muffled by colored glass. What kind of animal carried lamps with it.

A man.

A man could be a wild animal.

But why would he carry lamps or lanterns instead of a flashlight?

A madman?

And even if it were a man who was playing some grotesque hoax, wearing shoes that made those strange prints, he would not have been able to move so fast and put so much distance between us.

So where did that leave me?

Nowhere.

Standing at the end of the trail, staring out at the gray-white curtains of billowing flakes, I began to feel that the animal had circled behind me and now stood in my own footprints, watching me. The feeling grew so strong, so undeniable, that I whirled and cried out and stabbed my flashlight beam into the air behind me. But the night was all there was.

"You're being ridiculous," I told myself.

Having turned my back on the direction in which the animal had fled, uncomfortable because of that, I struggled through the ever-mounting drifts toward the rear of the farmhouse. I shone my flashlight ahead of me, even though I didn't need its light and would have been better off without it. Several times I thought I heard something out of place, a metallic snickering noise that I could not identify, nearby, above the ululation of the storm. But each time I probed the surrounding darkness with the flashlight, there was nothing to see but snow.

When I finally reached the house, brushed snow from my coat, and went into the sun porch, Connie was waiting for me. She said, "What was wrong?"

"I don't know."

She tilted her head to one side. "You found something. I can tell."

"I think it was that animal."

"The one whose tracks you found?"

"Yeah."

"Bothering the horses?"

"Yeah."

"Then you saw it?"

"No. But I found the tracks outside the stable window."

"Could you make anything of them this time?" she asked as she took my coat and hung it on the rack by the door. The ice-crusted hem and collar began to drip. Beads of bright water splashed on the floor.

"No," I said wearily. "I still couldn't make heads nor tails of them."

She took my scarf and shook the snow from it. "Did you follow them?" she asked.

I sat down on a pine bench and unzipped my boots, pulled them off, massaged my chilled toes. "Yeah, I followed them. For a few yards. Then they just vanished."

She took the boots and stood them in the corner beside her own and Toby's boots. "Well maybe it *is* a bird, like you said earlier."

"How do you figure?"

"A bird could have just taken off; he could have flown away, and that would explain why the prints vanished."

I shook my head: no. "This wind would tear his wings off. I don't see how a bird, any kind of bird at all, could be stalking about on a night like this."

"Or any other animal."

"Or any other animal," I agreed.

32

"Are the horses calmed down?"

"I don't hear them any more," I said.

"Do you think it'll be back—whatever it is?"

"Maybe. I don't know."

We stared at each other. Her perpetually startled eyes seemed even wider than usual. My eyes were probably wide too. We were frightened, and we didn't know why. No one had been hurt—or even threatened. We had seen nothing frightening. We had heard nothing frightening. It had done nothing more than scare the horses. But our fear was real, vague but indisputable: intuitive.

"Well," she said abruptly, "you were longer than I imagined you'd be. I'd better start dinner."

I drew her to me and hugged her. "Rotten horses."

"There's always later."

I kissed her.

She kissed back—and smiled when Toby called for us from the living room. "Later."

I released her, turned back to the sun porch door, and slid the bolt latch in place, although we usually left it unlocked. When we went through the kitchen door, I closed and locked that too.

4.

After dinner I went into the den and took from the shelves all the volumes that might conceivably help me to identify our mysterious new neighbor. Sitting behind the heavy, dark oak desk, a short brandy at hand, the empty gun cabinet at my back, I spent more than an hour paging through eight thick books, studying descriptions, drawings, and photographs of wildlife prints and spoors. With those animals whose marks I found altogether unfamiliar, I turned the examples on their sides and upside down, hoping to come across the prints that I was looking for simply by viewing these at odd angles. In some four hundred samples, however, there was nothing vaguely similar to what I had seen in the snow, regardless of the view that I took of them.

I was putting the books back on the shelves when Connie came into the den.

She said, "Any luck?"

"None."

"Why don't you come keep us company? Toby's working with his tempra paints, and I'm reading. I've got a pretty good FM station with lots of gutsy Rimsky-Korsakov mixed in with Beethoven."

I caught her up in my arms and lifted her off the floor and kissed her, tasting the minty tang of the after-dinner liqueur she had been drinking. She was the kind of woman a man wants to hold a great deal: feminine and yet not soft in any way, sensual yet not forbidding. Her father and her father's father had been bricklayers, yet there was a certain undeniable nobility in her face; she had the presence and the grace of one born to high position. It was inconceivable to me, just then, as I held her, that I had ever retreated from this part of reality, from Connie.

"Don, Toby is in the next room—"

I shushed her. "Dr. Cohen who is a psychiatrist and who ought to know all about these things, says that we should kiss and cuddle in front of Toby so that he knows we really love each other and so he doesn't think that I was away all that time because I *wanted* to be away." I kissed her again. "Therefore, this is not merely a bit of hot necking—it's psychiatric therapy for our entire family. Can you argue with that?"

She grinned. "I guess not."

Just then Toby knocked on the half-open den door and stepped cautiously across the threshold.

We broke apart, though not with haste, Connie's hand still on my arm. "Yes, Toby?"

He had been standing there, apparently, for long seconds, trying to decide how best to attract our attention without embarrassing us. He was strangely stiff, as if he were taking part in a good posture demonstration in school. His face was pale, his eyes very wide, and his mouth loose-lipped as if he were about to be ill.

Connie saw his condition even as I did, and we hurried over to him. She put a hand on his forehead and evidently decided there was no temperature. "What's the matter, Toby?"

36

He looked at me and then at her and then back at me again. Fat tears swelled at the corners of his eyes, but he made a valiant effort to keep from spilling them.

"Toby?" I said, kneeling beside him, caging him between Connie and me, caging him in love.

He said, "I can't . . ." He spoke in a whisper, and his voice trailed away into confusion.

She said, "What? Can't what, darling?"

He bit his lip. He was trembling.

To Connie I said, "He's scared to death."

"Toby?"

"I can't tell," he said.

"Why not?" Connie asked, smoothing his dark hair back from his forehead.

"I don't want to—to upset Dad," he said.

("There will be times," Dr. Cohen had said, that last day in his office before I was turned loose from the sanitarium, "when people—even those you love and who love you—will say things both intentionally and unintentionally, but most often the latter, that will remind you of your illness. They will hurt you, hurt you very badly. You'll be guilt-stricken for having abandoned your family. You'll want to crawl away somewhere and be by yourself, as if you're a wounded animal. However, being by yourself is unquestionably the worst medicine, Donald. Stay there. Face it. Push ahead with it. Do your best to conceal your wounds and try to salvage the situation." The doctor had known his business, all right.)

"You won't upset me, Toby," I said. The words were difficult to form and even more difficult to speak. "I'm perfectly all right now. I don't get upset very easily any more."

He stared at me, unblinkingly, trying to assess the

degree of truth in what I said. He had stopped trembling; he was utterly still.

"Go on," Connie said, holding him against her.

He could no longer restrain the tears. They slid down his round cheeks, glistening brightly, dripping from the soft line of his chin. He began to shudder—just as he shuddered when he tried to eat something that he didn't like in order to impress us with his manly fortitude.

"Toby?"

"Come on, Toby. Tell us."

"At the window," he said. It came out of him in a rush now, the words running together, expelled in gasping breaths. "At the window, right at the window, in the other room, I saw it at the living room window and it had yellow eyes."

Frowning, Connie said, "What had yellow eyes?"

"Big yellow eyes," he said, frightening himself even more as he recalled them. "It had big yellow eyes as big around as my whole hand, really big, looking straight at me." He held up his hand to show how big the eyes had been.

Connie looked at me, raised her eyebrows.

"I'm not lying," Toby said.

I said, "You both wait here."

"Don—" Connie began, reaching for me with her free hand.

I wasn't going to be restrained, for I remembered the pair of amber lights at the stable window. A child might have called them "yellow". At the time I had wondered what sort of an animal carried lamps or lanterns around with it, had decided that the only thing that did was a man, and had not considered any other explanation for those dual circles of light. And now Toby had given it to me: eyes.

But . . . eyes? Well, the eyes of many animals seemed to glow in the dark. Cats' eyes were green. And some of them, like the mountain lions and wildcats, had yellow eyes, amber eyes—didn't they?

Sure they did.

Yellow eyes.

But yellow eyes as big as saucers . . . ?

In the living room I looked quickly around at the three large windows but didn't see anything out of the ordinary. I went to each window then and stared through it at the brief view of snow-covered ground, darkness, and shifting, skipping snowflakes. Whatever Toby had seen, whether eyes or lanterns, man or animal, it was now long gone.

I recalled how fast it had moved away from the barn when I had set out after it . . .

Behind me, Connie and Toby came into the living room. He clung to her with one hand and wiped tears out of his eyes with the other hand. In a moment he would stop crying; in two moments he would smile; in three he would be recovered altogether. He was a tough little man; he had had to learn to rely on himself early in life.

"Which window was it?" I asked him.

He let go of Connie's hand and walked over toward the window that lay immediately to the left of the front door.

When I went to check it again, I thought to look down at the drifted bank of snow which had built up on the floor of the front porch—and I saw the prints. The same prints. Sharp, well defined holes in the snow. Eight holes in each grouping.

Connie sensed the new tension that blossomed inside of me. "What is it?"

I said, "Come and look."

39

She came; I showed her.

"Was it that animal again?" Toby asked. He crowded in between us, pressing his nose to the glass. He had stopped crying.

"I think it was," I said.

"Oh, that's all right then," he said.

"It is, huh?"

"Oh, sure. I thought it was something a whole lot worse than just some old animal." He was actually smiling now. Looking up at Connie, he said, "Can I have another piece of cake, Mom? My piece at supper wasn't very big."

She looked at him closely. "Are you feeling okay, Toby?"

"Just hungry," he said. The fear had dissipated like an electrical charge. He said, "It was only that animal. When the snow stops, tomorrow maybe, Dad and I are going to put on our snowshoes and track it down and find out what it is." When neither of us could think of a reply to that, Toby said, "Mom? The cake?"

"To be ten again," I said.

Connie laughed. She put one hand in Toby's mop of hair and messed it up, a show of affection he stolidly endured. "Come into the kitchen, me lad, where you can eat it without getting crumbs over everything."

I let them go. The whole time that Toby had his cake, I stood at the window and looked at those queer prints as the wind and the snow erased them.

5.

Later, when Toby was upstairs taking a bedtime bath and we were sitting on the sofa before the fireplace, Connie said, "Do you think you should—load the gun?"

When I had been drafted into the Army, Connie had purchased a .38 automatic which she had kept in the house for protection against burglars. We still had the pistol and the box of ammunition. In the army I had learned how to handle a gun; therefore, we weren't exactly unprepared.

"Load it?" I said. "Well . . . Not just yet."

"When?"

"Maybe it won't be necessary."

"But this animal might be dangerous."

"I don't think so," I said. "And even if it is dangerous, it can't get in the house all that easily."

"Well . . ."

"I don't like having a loaded gun lying around."

"I suppose you're right."

"It's not that I'm afraid to load the gun, Connie. If a time comes when I have to use it, I will. I'll be able to use it. I no longer feel that a gun, of itself, is evil. I've spent hundreds of hours with Dr. Cohen, you know. I can use a gun again without going to pieces."

41

"I *know* you can." She looked away from the crackling flames that enshrouded the birch logs. Her face was flushed and pretty.

"I think the first thing I should do is call Sam Caldwell and see if he can help me."

"Now?"

"It's as good a time as any."

"I'd better go up and see how Toby's getting along, make sure he brushes his teeth." When she reached the bottom of the stairs she looked back at me and said, "Don, you mustn't worry so much about what we think of you. We love you. We always will. We love you and trust you to take good care of us."

I nodded, and she smiled at me. I watched her climb the steps until she was out of sight, and I wished that I could trust myself as much as she trusted me. Would I, *could* I, load and use the pistol if the time came for that sort of action—or would the weapon remind me of the war, Southeast Asia, all of those things that I had fled into catatonia in order to forget? Would I be able to defend my family —or would I back off from the gun like a man backing off from a rattlesnake? I simply didn't know; and until I *did* know, I didn't deserve her smile.

In the den I dialed Sam Caldwell's number. It rang four times before he answered.

"Sam? Don Hanlon."

"You ready to be snowbound?" he asked.

"You think it'll come to that?"

"Sure do. Looks to me like we're in for the first big fall of the year."

"Well, I'm kind of looking forward to it."

"That's the proper attitude. Being snowbound is restful, peaceful."

I decided that was enough smalltalk. Neither of us

cared much for long discussions about the weather, politics, or religion. Sam, especially, was scornful of wasted words; he was very much a taciturn, friendly, but totally self-sufficient and self-contained New Englander.

He had come to the same conclusion a split second before I did. "What did you call for?" he asked in that brisk, short, but not impolite manner of his.

"You hunt quite a lot."

"That's true."

"Do you know the spore of the animals most likely to be roaming through these woods?"

"Sure do."

"All of them?"

"I've hunted nearly all of them."

"Well, I've come across something pretty unusual. I never saw prints like these—and I can't seem to find them in any of the books I have out here."

"You can't learn a wildcraft from a book."

"That's precisely why I called you."

"Shoot, then."

I gave him a detailed description of the prints. I started to tell him about the amber eyes, about the creature that had been at the stable window and at our living room window—but I was cut off when the lights went out and the phone went dead at the same instant.

"Sam?" I said, although I knew that the connection had been broken.

The only response was silence.

"Don!" Connie shouted.

I put the receiver in the cradle and felt my way out of the den into the living room. The darkness seemed total at first and was only gradually mitigated by the phosphorescent glow of the snow fields which

43

lay beyond the window and shone against the glass. "Are you all right?" I called to her.

"The lights are out," she said. Before I could respond to that she said, "Well, isn't that silly of me?" She laughed nervously. "You *know* the lights are out."

I could tell that, like me, she had been frightened by the sudden darkness. And, also like me, she had connected—initially and irrationally—the power failure with the yellow-eyed animal that had terrified the horses.

"The phone went dead too," I said.

"Did Sam have any idea what—"

"He didn't get a chance to say."

After a brief hesitation she said, "I'm going to get Toby bundled up in a robe and bring him downstairs."

"Don't try to get down the steps without a light," I said. "I'll find the candles in the kitchen and bring one up to you."

That was considerably easier said than done. We had lived in the house only a little longer than half a year, and I was not so familiar with its layout that I could find my way easily in the dark. Crossing the living room was not so bad; but the kitchen was a battleground, for it had only one window to let in the snow glare. I barked my shins on three of the four chairs that stood around the small breakfast table, cracked my hip on the heavy chrome handle of the oven door, and nearly fell over Toby's box of tempra paints which he had left on the floor in front of the cabinet where they were supposed to be kept. I tried four drawers before I finally found the candles and matches. I lit two candles, at the expense of a charred

44

thumb, and went back to the stairs in the living room, feeling rather foolish.

When he saw me Toby called down from the second-floor landing: "Hey, we're roughing it."

"Until we get the house's generator going," I said, climbing up toward them. "Maybe half an hour."

"Great!"

I led them down the steps in the dancing candle-light, and we went back into the kitchen where Connie found two brass holders to relieve me of the candles which had begun to melt and drip hotly on my hands.

"What happened?" she asked.

She was not taking the inconvenience with Toby's kind of high spirits.

Neither was I.

"The wind's just awful tonight," I said. "It probably brought down a tree somewhere along the line. Power and telephone cables are on the same poles— so one good-sized oak or maple or pine could do the whole job."

"Great!" Toby said. He looked at us, misinterpreted our glum expressions, and corrected himself. "I mean—fabulous!"

"I better go see about the generator," I said.

"What about fuel?" Connie asked.

"There's plenty of oil in the ground tank. We could run the house on our own power for a week or ten days without any problem."

"Swiss Family Robinson," Toby said.

"Well," I told him, "we have a few technological advantages that weren't available to the Swiss Family Robinson."

"You think it might be a week or ten days before the lines are restored?" Connie asked.

"No, no. I was on the phone with Sam when it happened. He'll know what's gone wrong. He'll call the telephone and the power companies. As soon as this blizzard lets up a bit, they'll start out to see about it."

Tony grabbed hold of my sleeve and tugged on it. "Hey, Dad! Can I go out to the generator with you?"

"No," Connie said.

"But why, Mom?"

"You just had a bath."

"What's that got to do with it?" Plaintively.

"A hot bath opens your pores," she told him, "and makes you susceptible to colds. You'll stay in here with me."

But we both knew that was not the real reason he would have to stay inside rather than go with me to the barn where the auxiliary generator was stored.

You're being irrational, I told myself.

The yellow-eyed animal had nothing to do with this.

Maybe . . .

Why do you fear it so much? You haven't seen it. It hasn't tried to harm you. Instinct? That's not good enough. Well, it's as if the thing, whatever it is, emanates some sort of radiation that generates fear . . . But that isn't good enough either; in fact, that's downright silly.

It's only an animal.

Nothing more.

Yes. Of course. But what if . . .

What if *what?*

I couldn't answer that one.

"I'll get your coat and boots," Connie said.

I picked up one of the candles. "I'm going to the den for a minute."

46

She turned around, silhouetted in the orange candlelight, her blue eyes touched with green. What—"

"To get the pistol. It's time to load it."

6.

For the first time in weeks, I dreamed. It was a replay of the old, once-familiar nightmare:

I was pinned down by enemy rifle fire, lying in a meager patch of scrub brush, forty yards from the base of the long slope that was referred to on ordnance maps as Hill #898. The flatland that we held was swampy; the rain fell hard and fast, impacting with an endless *snap!snap!snap!* on the vegetation and on my fatigues. When it struck my face, it stung as if it were a swarm of insects.

A bullet would feel the same as the droplets of rain felt: a brief and surprisingly sharp sting, a minute convulsion, nothing more. The only interesting difference would be in what took place afterwards. If it were a bullet instead of a raindrop, then perhaps nothing at all would take place afterwards, nothing whatsoever, only endless emptiness.

Through the flat, shiny leaves of the waist-high dwarf jungle, I had an excellent view of the crest of the hill where the Cong had dug in. Now and again something moved up there, soliciting a burst of fire from our own positions. Otherwise, it was like a gray-green skull, that hill, featureless and dead and unspeakably alien. The rain washed down over it; thick fingers of mist sometimes obscured the summit; yet it did not seem possible that it could be a natural piece of this landscape. It looked, instead, as if it had come from some other world or time and had been dropped here on the whim of a celestial Power.

When the attack finally came the scene was even less real than it had been before: twisted, grotesque, shifting and changing like a face in a funhouse mirror.

There were thirty-seven of us in the thick tangle of rubbery plants, awaiting helicopter-borne reinforcements. More than a hundred and fifty of the enemy held Hill #898, and they had made the decision that we had all been afraid they would make: it was best for them if they overran us, wiped us out, and then dealt with the helicopters when they tried to land.

They came.

Screaming . . .

That was the worst of it. They came down that hill with no regard for our return fire, a wave of them, their front ranks armed with machine guns that were used most effectively, the men in the second and third ranks holding their rifles over their heads and screaming, screaming wordlessly. In seconds, before more than a score of them could be brought down, they had gained the brush: the situation had deteriorated into hand-to-hand combat.

The moment they had started down the hill, I had torn the sheet of thin, transparent plastic—like a dry cleaner's bag—from my rifle and let the rain hit it for the first time. But the screams so paralyzed me that I couldn't fire. Screams, distorted yellow faces, the mist, the torrential rain, the tooth of Hill #898,

50

the rubbery plants . . . If I fired at them, I would be admitting that the entire thing was *real*. I was not up to that just yet.

When they were upon us, I stumbled to my feet, jarred out of the dangerous trance by a sudden and awful awareness of my mortality. Four of the enemy seemed maniacally determined to destroy me, no one else, just me, me alone, as if I were some personal enemy of theirs and not just any American. I caught the first of them with a shot through the chest, blew off the face of the second one, opened the stomach of the third, and placed two shots in the chest of the last man. Two shots: the first did not stop him. It had been in the center of his chest, heart-center, yet he came forward as if he were an automaton. The second bullet jerked him to the left and slowed him down considerably, but it did not stop him either. A half-breath later, he slammed into me. The thin blade of his rifle bayonet ripped through my shoulder, bringing lightning with it, pain like lightning, sharp and bright. We both went down in the wet scrub brush—and I blacked out.

When I came to, the world was utterly silent, without even the voice of the rain.

Something heavy bore down on me, and I felt curiously numb. But I was alive. Wasn't I? That was something, anyway. That was really something. Wasn't it?

I opened my eyes and found that the dead soldier lay atop me. His head was on my left shoulder, his face turned towards me. His black eyes were open, as was his mouth. He looked as if he were still screaming.

I tried to push him off, cried out as an intense

51

wave of pain gushed down the right side of my body, and collapsed back against the soggy earth.

Carefully I turned my head away from him and looked at my right shoulder where the bayonet had driven all the way through and into the earth beneath me. The dead man's hands had slipped down until they clenched the end of the barrel where the haft of the knife was affixed. I tried to reach across the body and pry those fingers loose. They were coiled so tightly around the weapon that I could not move them, not as weak and frightened as I was. Each time I made another attempt to shake off the body or free the bayonet, the blood bubbled out of my wound and soaked the sleeve of my shirt. Already, I was drawing ants.

We lay there for eleven hours. The ants came and scouted my face and chose to let me go until I died. They crawled inside the yellow man's open mouth and clustered over his eyes. I didn't want to watch them, yet I found myself staring helplessly. Time stretched into weeks and months: minutes became hours, time was distorted, appeared to slow down—yet I seemed to be careening at a frightening speed down a narrow tube of time, toward a round black exit into nothingness.

Screaming . . .

This time it was me.

I remembered the other three men I had killed, and my mind filled with images of rotting corpses, although I could not see them from where I lay. Four men . . . So what? I had killed a dozen men on other missions.

Screaming . . .

Now stop it, I told myself.

But I couldn't stop.

52

I might have killed a dozen men before this—but they had not seemed like men to me. The killing had been done from a distance, and I had been able to think of my targets as, simply, "the enemy". That made it impersonal, acceptable. Euphemisms made it seem like little more than target practice. But now, lying here in the scrub, I could not avoid the truth, could not avoid the fact that these were men I had killed. I saw my own sin—and my own mortality—in vivid terms. I saw that these were men, saw the undeniable truth, because I was looking directly into one of their faces (and Death looking back at me), looking into an open mouth full of bad teeth (and Death grinning in the rictus), looking at an earlobe that had been pierced for a ring that wasn't there now (and Death holding the ring out to me in one bony hand), looking at chapped lips . . .

When they found me eleven hours later, I asked them to please kill me.

The medic said, "Nonsense." The chattering helicopter blades made his words sound disjointed, mechanical. "You've been badly hurt, but you're well enough. You're incredibly lucky!"

And then the dream began all over again. I was lying in scrub brush at the bottom of Hill #898, waiting for the enemy to attack, my rifle wrapped in plastic—

I woke, coated with perspiration, my hands full of twisted sheets and blankets.

In real life the battle for Hill #898 had happened only once, of course. But at night when I dreamed, it played over and over and over like a film loop in my mind. That was, however, the only important difference between the reality and the remembrance.

53

All the ingredients of a nightmare had been there in the genuine event; there was, therefore, no need for me to add anything to sharpen the horror.

Beside me, Connie slept unaware of any struggling that I may have done in my effort to wake up.

I got quietly out of bed and went to the window to see if the storm had abated at all. It had not. If anything, the wind pressed against the house more fiercely than ever, and the snow was falling half again as hard as it had been when I went outside to start the auxiliary generator. More than twelve inches of new snow sheathed the world. The drifts had been whipped up to five and six feet in many places.

As I studied the night and the snow I realized, once again, how vulnerable was our position. The generator—which supplied the electricity to light the house and the stable, run our appliances, and keep the two oil furnaces going—was not particularly well protected from vandalism. One need only force the stable doors and take a wrench to the machinery. We would be forced to huddle around the fireplace, sleeping and eating within the radius of its warmth, until help arrived.

That might be several days from now—even a week.

And in that time anything could happen.

But I was being childish again. There was no— what? monster? monster, for god's sake?—monster out there in the snow. It was a dumb beast. It would have no conception of the purpose of the generator. There was nothing to fear.

Then why was I afraid?

For a moment I thought I felt something—like cold fingers—grasping at the back of my mind. I tried to recoil from the sensation, realized it was within me, and almost collapsed from sheer terror. Then, abruptly, the sensation passed: but the fear remained.

As I looked out on the storm and over the snow-draped land, I was aware of an *alien* quality to all of it, something not unlike the eerie unreality that I had sensed while lying at the bottom of Hill #898 waiting for the battle to begin again. If I had not been out in that foul weather, I would have considered the notion that it was all a stage setting, carefully crafted of cardboard and paint and rice. There was too much snow, too much wind, too bitter cold for reality. This white world was the home of other entities, not of man. It tolerated man, nothing more.

The irrational fear swelled in me again.

I tried to choke it down; it almost choked me instead.

This is Maine, I told myself as firmly as I could. And that thing out there is only an animal, not something supernatural or even supernormal. Just an animal. Probably native to this area—but, at worst, an animal that has escaped from a zoo. That's all.

That's all.

Connie murmured in her sleep. She twisted from side to side and mumbled in what sounded like a foreign language.

Wind moaned at the glass in front of me.

Connie sat straight up in bed and called my name. "Don! Don, don't let it near me! Don't let it have me!"

I went to her, but even as I reached for her shoulders she collapsed back against her pillows. In an instant the dream had left her, and she was sleeping peacefully.

I sat on the edge of the bed and picked up the gun from the nightstand. It was loaded; I had filled the magazine myself. Nevertheless, I checked it again to be sure before I leaned back against my pillows to wait for something to happen.

THURSDAY

The Fear

7.

At nine o'clock the next morning, just after break-fast, I used the lawn mower-sized snow blower to clear a narrow path between the house and the barn. The machine sounded like a jet fighter entering a power dive. Numbing vibrations jolted along my arms and across my shoulders and back down my arms into the snow blower's handles from which they had come, like electricity flowing through a closed circuit. The snow shot up and out and away to my right in a dazzling, sparkling crescent.

Snow was falling only lightly now, and the wind had quieted considerably. Eighteen inches of new snow was on the ground, but that wasn't going to be the end of it. The sky was still low and leaden; and according to the radio reports out of Bangor—to which we had listened during breakfast—a second storm front, even worse than the first one which had not yet quite finished passing over us, had moved into the area. The snow and wind might have gentled for the time being, but they would be raging again by late this afternoon, no doubt about it.

In fifteen minutes I had opened the path, and I switched off the machine. The winter silence fell in over me like collapsing walls of cotton. For a moment I was too stunned to hear anything at all. Gradually

I began to perceive the soft whistle of the wind and the rustling branches of the big Douglas fir which stood at the corner of the barn.

"Dad, isn't it great? Isn't it?"

Toby had run over from the house to join me the moment I shut off the snow blower. He was supposed to be in the kitchen studying his lessons right now. Connie was an elementary school teacher by trade and had been granted a limited state license to act as Toby's tutor so long as we lived on Timberlake Farm. She kept him to a fairly strict study schedule, administering one state-prepared exam a week in order to monitor his progress. However, she had slept badly last night, and Toby had been able to con her into a brief postponement of this morning's session so that he could come with me while I watered, fed, and walked our horses.

Grinning out at the white world, barely able to see over the wall of snow I'd thrown up on the right side of the path, he said, "Did you ever see so much snow at one time?"

I stared down along the pale slope toward the pine forest that was dressed in snow and laces of ice. It was a glittering, pain-bright scene. "No, Toby, I never did."

"Let's have a snowball fight," he said.

"Later, maybe. First there's work to do."

I went to the barn door and pulled back the ice-crusted bolt latch, slid open the door.

Toby ran past me into the dimly lighted barn.

I went inside and headed straight for the corner where I kept the grain bins and tools.

As I was taking a bucket down from the wall peg on which it hung, Toby said, "Dad?"

"Yeah?" I asked as I put the bucket under the

water faucet that came out of the floor beside the grain bin.

"Where's Blueberry?"

"What?"

"Where's Blueberry?"

"What are you talking about?"

"Dad?"

I straightened up and looked at him. He was standing halfway down the stable row, directly in front of an open stall door, Blueberry's stall. He was staring at me and frowning hard; and his lips were trembling.

He said, "Blueberry's gone."

"Gone?"

He looked into the empty stall.

Abruptly, I was aware of how *wrong* things were in the barn. The horses were inordinately quiet: deathly quiet and still. Kate was standing in the third stall on the left, her head hung low over the door, not watching me, not watching Toby, gazing blankly at the straw-strewn floor in the stable row. Betty was lying on her side in the next stall down the line; I could see her blunt black nose protruding from the gap under the stall's half-door. Furthermore, there was a peculiar odor in the air: ammonia, something like ammonia, but not unpleasant, vague and sweet, sweet ammonia . . .

And Blueberry had vanished.

What in the hell is going on? I wondered.

Deep inside I knew. I just didn't want to admit it.

I walked over to Kate and quietly said her name. I expected her to rear back and whinny in alarm, but she had no energy for that sort of thing. She just slowly raised her head and stared at me, stared through me, looking very dull and stupid and empty.

61

I stroked her face and scratched her ears; and she snuffled miserably. All of the spirit had gone out of her; during the night something had happened which had utterly broken her, for good and for always.

But what had it been? I asked myself.

You know exactly what it was, I answered.

The yellow-eyed animal?

Yes.

You think it stole Blueberry?

Yes.

Couldn't Blueberry have escaped on her own?

If she did, then she was thoughtful enough to stop and latch the bolt behind her. The door was closed and locked.

There's some other explanation.

There's no other explanation.

I put an end to this tense but useless interior monologue as I opened the door to Betty's stall and knelt beside her.

Betty was dead. I stroked her neck and found that it was cold and stiff. Dried sweat, in the form of a salt crust, streaked her once-sleek coat. The air in the stall was redolent of urine and manure. Her brown eyes bulged, as if about to pop loose of the sockets. Her lips were drawn back from her teeth. She looked as if she had died of fright.

I stood up and closed the stall door before Toby caught sight of the grisly corpse.

"We've got to find Blueberry," he said, closing the open door to her stall.

I took him by the shoulder and led him down the stable row toward the barn door. "*You've* got to get back to the house and work on your math and history lessons. I'll find Blueberry."

He stopped and pulled away from me and said, "I want to go with you."

"You've got to study."

"I can't study."

"Toby—"

"I'll worry about Blueberry."

"There's nothing to worry about," I said.

"Where will you look?"

"I'll search along the lane. And out on the north fields. And then down near the woods—and in the woods. I'll find her one place or the other."

"Why would she run away?"

"She was frightened by the wind. When I was in here last evening, the wind was rattling the window and moaning over the roof, whistling in the eaves . . . The horses were frightened even then, and the storm got worse during the night."

"If she was frightened of the storm," he said, "she wouldn't run out into it."

"She might. Horses aren't really too bright."

"She didn't run away," he insisted.

"Well, she's gone."

"Someone took her."

"Stole her?"

"Yeah."

"Nonsense, Toby."

He was adamant.

"Why would he steal just one horse when there were three?"

"I don't know."

The window rattled in its frame.

Nothing: just the wind.

Startled, trying to cover my uneasiness, glancing at the empty window and remembering the twin amber discs that I had seen there last evening, I said, "Who would do a thing like that? Who would come here and steal your pony?"

He shrugged.

63

"Well, whatever the case, I'll find her," I promised him, wondering if I could keep the promise, fairly sure that I could not. "I'll find her."

* * *

Shortly after ten o'clock I left the farmhouse again. This time I had the loaded pistol in my right coat pocket.

The sky had grown subtly darker, more somber, a deeper shade of gunmetal blue-gray than it had been only an hour ago.

Or was it merely my outlook that had darkened?

From where I stood on the crown of the hill, there were three ways I could go, three general areas in which I could search for Blueberry: along the narrow private lane that connected with the county road two miles away, or in and around the open fields that lay to the west and south of the house, or in the forest which lay close at hand on the north and east of us. If Blueberry had run away of her own accord (somehow locking the barn door behind her) she would be out in the open fields. If a *man* had come to steal her, the place to look for clues would be along the lane, out in the direction of the highway. Therefore, not wanting to waste any time, I turned away from the lane and the fields and walked straight down the hill toward the waiting forest.

At the edge of the woods I took a deep breath. I listened and heard nothing and listened some more and finally let out the breath. Plumes of white vapor rose in front of my face. I passed through them as if I were entering a room through a gauzy curtain.

I walked among the trees, crossed frozen puddles, stumbled through patches of snow-concealed briars and brambles and ground vines. I crossed gullies where powdery snow lay deep over a soft mulch of rotting autumn leaves. I climbed wooded hills and passed ice-draped bushes that glinted rainbowlike. I stomped across an iron-hard frozen stream, stepped unwittingly into deep drifts from which I fought to extricate myself, and went on . . .

After a while I stopped, not sure at first why I stopped—and gradually realized that something was wrong here. My always-working subconscious mind sensed it first, but now I began to get a conscious hold on it. Something . . .

I panted, trying to regain my breath and energy. I sniffed the air—and there it was, the *wrongness*, finally defined: ammonia, a vague but unmistakable and undeniable odor, ammonia and yet not ammonia, too sweet for ammonia, sweet ammonia, the same thing that I had smelled in the barn just two hours ago when Toby had first said that Blueberry was missing.

I took the pistol out of my coat pocket and flicked off the safety. My pigskin gloves were unlined, and they did not interfere with my grip or with my hold on the trigger.

Tense, my shoulders hunched, chin tucked down, heart thudding, I looked to my left, to my right, ahead, behind, and even above me. Nothing. I was alone.

Proceeding with considerably more caution than I had shown thus far, I followed the crest of the wooded hill, followed the growing ammonia scent. I descended a gentle slope into a natural cathedral whose walls were ranks of pine tree trunks and whose vaulted ceiling was made of arching pine boughs.

The boughs were so thickly interlaced that only

two or three inches of snow had sifted to the floor of the clearing. And what snow there was had been trampled by the animal. There were literally hundreds of the curious eight-hole prints in the clearing.

The only other thing in the clearing worth mentioning was Blueberry.

What was left of Blueberry.

Not much.

Bones.

I stood over the skeleton—which was certainly that of a small horse—staring down at it, unable to see how this was possible. The bones were stained yellow and brown—but not a single scrap of flesh or gristle adhered to them. They had been stripped clean. And yet there was no blood or gore in the snow around them. It was as if Blueberry had been dipped into a huge vat of sulphuric acid. But where was the vat? What had happened here? Had the yellow-eyed animal—God bless us—had the yellow-eyed animal *eaten* an entire young horse?

Impossible!

Insane!

I looked around at the purple-black shadows beneath the trees, and I held the pistol out in front of me.

The odor of ammonia was very strong. It was choking me. I felt dizzy, slightly disoriented.

What sort of creature could eat a horse, pick the bones bare, leave it like this? I wanted to know; more than anything else in the world I wanted to know. I stared into the trees, desperately searching for a clue, thinking: *What is out there, what is this thing, what am I up against?*

Suddenly I was sure that it was trying to answer me. I felt a curious pressure against my eyes and then against my entire skull. And then the pressure was not outside pressing in: it was *in*, moving inside my mind, whirling, electric. Patterns of light danced behind my eyes. An image began to form, an image of the yellow-eyed animal, shadowy and indistinct at first but clearing, clearing—

—and fear exploded in me like a hand grenade exploding in a trench, obliterating the image before it could finish forming. All of a sudden, I was unable to tolerate this intimate invasion. It disturbed me on a subconscious-unconscious level, deep down where I had no control over myself. Something was crawling around inside my skull, something that seemed hairy and damp, slithering over the wet surface of my brain, trying to find a place to dig in. It was useless of me to try to convince myself that this was not the case, for I was responding viscerally now, like a primitive, like a wild beast. Something was in my skull, a many-legged thing. Unthinkable! Get it out! Now! Out! I fought back, thrust the force out of me, tried to keep it from seeping back into me. I threw punches at the air and screamed and twisted as if I were battling with a physical rather than a mental adversary.

Diamond-hard fear . . . nameless horror . . . irrational terror . . . my heart thundering, nearly rupturing with each colossal beat . . . the taste of bile . . . my breath trapped in my throat . . . a scream trapped in my throat . . . sweat streaming down my face . . . unable to cry out for help and no one to help even if I could cry out to them . . . a balloon swelling and swelling inside my chest, bigger, bigger, going to burst . . .

I turned away from the skeleton, fell and cracked my chin, scrambled to my feet.

The mysterious pressure clinging around my head increased, slipped inside of me again, and began to work up the yellow-eyed image once more . . .

Out!

I ran. I had never run in the war; I had stood up to anything and everything. Even my mental illness, my catatonia, had not been the product of fear; I had been driven, then, by disillusionment and self-loathing. But now I ran, terrified.

I tore off my cap, pulled at my hair as if I were a raving lunatic, tried to grab and throttle whatever invisible being was trying to get inside of me.

I tripped over a log, went down, hard. But I got up, spitting blood and snow, and I climbed the side of a small hill.

I found my voice somewhere along the way. A scream burst from me. It echoed back to me from the crowding trees and hillsides. It didn't sound like my voice, although it surely was. It didn't even sound human.

For a long while—exactly how long, I really don't know, perhaps half an hour or perhaps twice that long—I weaved without direction through the forest. I remember running until my lungs were on fire, crawling like an animal, slithering on my belly, moaning and mumbling and gibbering senselessly. I had been driven temporarily insane by an unimaginably strong fear, a racial fear, an almost *biological* fear of the creature that had tried to contact me in that pine-circled clearing.

At last I tripped and fell face-down in a drift of snow, and I was unable to regain my feet or to crawl or even to slither on my belly any farther. I lay there, waiting to have the flesh picked from my bones . . .

As I regained my breath and as my heartbeat slowed, the biological fear subsided to be replaced by a more rational, much more manageable fear. My senses returned; my thoughts began to move once again, sluggishly at first, then like quick fishes. There was no longer anything trying to force its way inside of my head. I was alone in the quiet forest, watched over by nothing more sinister than the sentinel pines, lying on a soft bed of snow. I stared up at the darkening sky which issued fat, slowly twirling snowflakes, and I caught a few flakes on my tongue. For the moment, at least, I was safe.

Safe from what?

I had no answer for that one.

Safe for how long?

No answer.

As a bizarre thought occurred to me, I closed my eyes for all of a minute and opened them again only to see the sky, trees, and snow. Incredibly, I had half-expected to see hospital walls. For one awful moment I had thought that the farm and the forest and the yellow-eyed animal were not real at all but were only figments of my imagination, fragments of a dream verging on a nightmare, and that I was still in a deep catatonic trance, lying in a hospital room, helpless.

I shuddered. I had to get moving, or I was going to go all to pieces.

Weak from all of the running I had done, I struggled to my feet and found that I was still holding tightly to the pistol. My hand had formed like a frozen claw around it. I hesitated for a moment, glanced at the woods that crowded in all around me, awaited for something to attack me, decided that there was nothing nearby, and then put the gun in my coat pocket.

But I kept my hand on it.

I took half a dozen steps, stopped, whirled, and looked back at the peaceful wildlands. Biting my lip, forcing myself not to turn every time the wind moaned behind me, I started to find the way out of there.

Ten minutes later I reached the perimeter of the woods and began to climb the hill toward the farmhouse. In the middle of the slope, I stopped and turned and looked back at the trees. The snow had begun to fall as heavily and as fast as it had done all last evening; and the trees were hazy, indistinct, even though they were only fifty or sixty yards away. Nevertheless, I could see well enough to be sure that there was nothing down there at the edge of the forest, nothing that might have followed me. And then, as if my thoughts had produced it, a brilliant purple light flashed far away in the forest, at least a mile away, but purpling the snow around me in spite of the distance, flashed three times in quick succession like the revolving beam of a lighthouse, only three times and nothing more.

I watched. Nothing? Imagination? No, I had seen it; I was not losing my mind.

I waited.

Snow fell.

The wind picked up.

I tucked my chin down deeper in my neck scarf.

Darkness lowered behind the clouds.

Nothing . . .

At last I turned and walked up the hill to the house.

What the hell was happening here?

8.

At first I thought I would tell Toby that I hadn't been able to find a trace of Blueberry—reserving the full story for Connie. However, when I had a few minutes to think about it—as I stripped off my coat and boots, and as I thankfully clasped my hands around a mug of coffee laced with anisette—I decided not to shield him from the truth. After all he was a strong boy, accustomed to adversity, especially emotional adversity which was much more difficult to bear than any physical suffering; and I was confident that he could handle just about any situation better than other children his age. Besides, over the past several months I had worked at getting him to trust me, to have confidence in me, confidence deep down on a subconscious level where it really mattered; and now if I lied to him, I very well might shatter that confidence, shatter it so badly that it could never be rebuilt. Therefore, I told both him and Connie about Blueberry's fleshless skeleton which I had found in that forest clearing.

Surprisingly, he seemed neither frightened nor particularly upset. He shook his head and looked smug and said, "This is what I already expected."

Connie said. "What do you mean?"

"The animal ate Blueberry," Toby said.

"Oh, now——"

"I think he's right," I said.

She stared at me.

"There's more to come, and worse," I said. "But I'm not crazy. Believe me, I've considered that possibility, considered it carefully. But there are several undeniable facts: those strange tracks in the snow, the yellow-eyed thing at the window, Blueberry's disappearance, the bones in the clearing——none of that is the product of my imagination. Something——ate our pony. There is no other explanation, so far as I can see."

"Crazy as it may be," Connie said.

"Crazy as it may be."

Toby said, "Maybe there really is an old grizzly bear running around out there."

Connie reached out and took one of his hands away from his cup of cocoa. "Hey, you don't seem too upset for having just lost your pony."

"Oh," he said, very soberly, "I knew when I first came back from the barn that the animal had eaten Blueberry. I went right upstairs and cried about it then. I got over that. There's nothing I can do about it, so I got to live with it." His lips trembled a bit, but he didn't cry. As he had said, he was finished with that.

"You're something," I said.

He smiled at me, pleased. "I'm no crybaby."

"Just so you know it's not shameful to cry."

"Oh, I know," he said. "The only reason I did it in my room was because I didn't want anyone to kid me out of it until I was good and finished."

I looked at Connie. "Ten years old?"

"I truly believe he's a midget," she said, as pleased with him as I was.

Toby said, "Are we going to go out and track down that old grizzly bear, Dad?"

"Well," I said, "I don't think it is a grizzly bear."

"Some kind of bear."

"I don't think so."

"Mountain lion?" he asked.

"No. A bear or a mountain lion—or just about any other wild, carnivorous animal—would have killed the horse there in the barn and would have eaten it on the spot. We would have found blood in the barn, lots of it. A bear or a mountain lion wouldn't have killed Blueberry without leaving blood at the scene, wouldn't have carried her all the way down into the forest before it had supper."

"Then what is it?" Connie asked. "What is big enough to carry off a pony? And leave a whistle-clean skeleton. Do you have any ideas, Don?"

I hesitated. Then: "I have one."

"Well?"

"You won't like it. *I* don't like it."

"Nevertheless, I *have* to hear it," she said.

I sipped my coffee, trying to get my thoughts arranged, and finally I told them all about the flashing purple light in the woods and, more importantly, about the force that had attempted to take control of my mind. I minimized my fear-reaction in the retelling and made it sound as if the takeover attempt had been relatively easy to resist. There was no need to dramatize it, for even when it was underplayed and told in a lifeless monotone, the story was quite frightening.

I had recounted these events with such force and so vividly that Connie knew I was telling the truth—at least, the truth as I saw it—and that I was entirely serious. She still had trouble accepting it. She shook her head slowly and said, "Don, do you realize exactly what you're saying?"

"Yes."

"That this animal, this yellow-eyed thing that can devour a pony, is—*intelligent?*"

"That seems to be the most logical conclusion—as illogical as it may seem."

"I can't get a hold on it," she said.

"Neither can I. Not a good one."

Toby looked back and forth, from Connie to me to Connie to me again, as if he were doing the old routine about a spectator at a tennis match. He said, "You mean it's a space monster?"

We were all quiet for a moment.

I took a sip of coffee.

Finally Connie said, "*Is* that what you mean?"

"I don't know," I said. "I'm not sure . . . But it's a possibility we simply can't rule out."

More silence.

Then, Connie: "What are we going to do?"

"What *can* we do?" I asked. We're snowbound. The first big storm of the year—and one of the worst on record. We don't have a working telephone. We can't drive into town for help; even the microbus would get bogged down within a hundred yards of the house. So . . . We just have to wait and see what happens next."

She didn't like that, but then neither did I. She turned her own coffee mug in circles on the table top. "But if you're right, or even only half right, and if this thing can take control of our minds—"

"It can't," I said, trying to sound utterly confident even while remembering how perilously close the thing had come to taking control of mine. "It tried that with me, but it didn't succeed. We can resist it."

"But what else might it be able to do?"

"I don't know. Nothing else. Anything else."

"It might have a ray gun," Toby said enthusiastically.

"Even that's possible," I said. "As I said before, we'll just have to wait and see."

"This is really exciting," Toby said, not disturbed in the least by our helplessness.

"Maybe we won't see anything more of it," I said. "Maybe it will just go away."

But none of us believed that.

We talked about the situation for quite some time, examining all the possibilities, trying to prepare ourselves for any contingency, until there wasn't anything more to say that we hadn't already said a half a dozen times. Weary of the subject, we went on to more mundane affairs, as I washed the coffee and cocoa mugs while Connie began to prepare supper. It seemed odd, yet it was rather comforting, that we were able to deal with every-day affairs in the face of our most extraordinary circumstances. Only Toby was unable to get back to more practical matters; all he wanted to do was stand at the window, watch the forest, and wait for the "monster" to appear.

We allowed him to do as he wished, perhaps because we knew that there was no chance of our getting him interested in anything else, especially not in his lessons. Or perhaps both Connie and I felt that it wasn't really such a bad idea to have a sentry on duty.

As I was drying and shelving the mugs, Connie said, "What are we going to do about old Kate?"

"I forgot all about her!" I said. "After I found Betty dead and Blueberry missing, I didn't take time to feed and water her."

"That's the least of her problems," Connie said. "Even well fed and watered, she's not going to be safe out there tonight."

I thought about that for a moment and then said, "I'll bring her in on the sun porch for the night."

"That'll be messy."

"Yes, but at least we can watch over her and see she doesn't come to any harm."

"There's no heat on the sun porch."

"I'll move a space heater in from the barn. Then I'll be able to switch off the heat in the barn and let the temperature drop below freezing out there. That'll keep the dead horse from decomposing and becoming a health hazard."

I bundled up in coat, scarf, gloves, and boots once more and went out into the howling storm which was, by now, every bit as fierce as the storm we had suffered the previous day. Wind-whipped snow stung my face, and I squinted like an octogenarian trying to read a newspaper without his bifocals. Slipping, stumbling, wind-milling my arms, I managed to stay on my feet for the length of the path which I had opened this morning but which had already drifted most of the way shut.

In the new snow around the barn door, I found fresh examples of the strange eight-holed prints.

I began to sweat in spite of the bitterly cold air.

My hands shaking uncontrollably, I slid back the bolt and threw open the door and staggered into the barn. I knew what I would find. But I could not simply turn away and run back to the house without being absolutely certain that I was correct.

The barn was full of warm odors: hay, straw, manure, horse linament, the tang of well-used leather saddles, the dusty aroma of the grain in the feed bins

—and most of all, ammonia, dammit, sweet ammonia, so thick that it gagged me.

Kate was gone.

Her stall door stood open.

I ran down the stable row to Betty's stall and opened the half-door. The dead horse was where it had been, staring with glassy eyes: the yellow-eyed animal was apparently only interested in fresh meat.

Now what?

Before the scouring wind and the heavily falling snow could erase the evidence, I went outside to study the tracks again. This time, on closer inspection, I saw that Kate had left the barn under her own power: her hoof prints led down toward the forest. But of course! If the alien—yes, even as awkward as that sounded, it was still the only proper word—if the *alien* could come so close to seizing control of a human mind, how simple for it to mesmerize a dumb animal. Denied will power, the horse had gone off with the alien.

When I looked closer and after I followed the trail for a few yards, I corrected myself and added an "s" to the noun: aliens. Clearly, there had been at least two of them, probably three.

Numbed, I went back into the barn and turned off the heaters in order to keep the dead horse from decomposing. When I left I locked the door, although that was a pointless gesture now.

I looked at the tracks for a long while. Nightmarish thoughts passed through my mind like a magician's swords passing through the lady in a magic cabinet: Blueberry hadn't been supper, but lunch. Kate was their supper. What would they want for breakfast? Me? Connie? Toby? All three of us?

No.

Ridiculous.

Would the first encounter between man and alien be played out like some simple-minded movie, like a cheap melodrama, like a hack science fiction writer's inept plot: starman the gourmand, man the hapless meal?

We had to make sure that it did not go like that. We had to establish a communications bridge between these creatures and ourselves, a bridge to understanding.

Unless *they* didn't want to understand, didn't want to bother, didn't want anything from us except the protein that we carried in our flesh and blood . . .

I went back to the house, wondering if I were, indeed, out of my mind.

9.

Connie and I agreed to take turns standing guard duty during the night. She would sleep—or try to sleep—from ten o'clock until four the next morning, and then I would sleep—maybe—from around four until whatever time I woke up. We also agreed that we were basically a couple of real ninnies, that we were being overly cautious, that such an extreme safety measure as this was probably not necessary—yet neither of us suggested that we forget about the guard duty and just sleep together, unprotected, as we would have done any other night.

I helped her put Toby to bed shortly before ten, kissed her goodnight, and went to sit at the head of the stairs, in the precisely precribed circle of light from a tensor lamp. One table lamp was burning down in the living room, a warm yellow light that threw softly rounded shadows. The loaded pistol was at my side.

I was ready.

Outside, the storm wind fluted under the eaves and made the rafters creak.

I picked up a paperback novel and tried to get interested in a sympathetic professional thief who was masterminding a bank robbery in New Orleans. It seemed to be an exciting, well told story; my eyes fled along the lines of print; the pages passed quickly; but I didn't retain more than five percent of what I read. Still, I stayed with it, for there was no better way to get through the next six hours.

The trouble came sooner than I had expected. Twenty-three minutes past eleven o'clock. I knew the precise time because I had just looked at my wristwatch. I was no more than one-third of the way through the paperback novel, having absorbed little or nothing of it, and I was getting bored.

Gentle, all but inaudible footsteps sounded in the second-floor hallway behind me, and when I turned around Toby was there in his bare feet and fire-engine-red pajamas.

"Can't you sleep?" I asked.

He said something: an incoherent gurgle, as if someone were strangling him.

"Toby?"

He came down onto the first step, as if he were going to sit beside me—but instead of that he slipped quickly past me and kept right on going.

"What's up?" I asked, thinking that he was headed for the refrigerator to get a late-night snack.

He didn't answer.

He didn't stop.

"Hey!"

He started to run down the last of the steps.

I stood up. "Toby!"

At the bottom of the stairs he glanced up at me. And I realized that there was no expression whatsoever in his eyes. Just a watery emptiness, a vacant gaze, a lifeless stare. He seemed to be looking through me at the wall beyond, as if I were only a spirit drifting on the air.

One of the aliens had control of him.

Why had it never occurred to me that the aliens might find a child's mind much more accessible, much more controllable than the mind of an adult?

As Toby ran across the living room, I started down the stairs, taking them two at a time, risking a twisted ankle and a broken neck. As I ran I shouted at him, hoping that somehow my voice would snap him out of the trance.

He kept going.

Bones . . . bones . . . a horse's bones, a complete skeleton . . . bones in a forest clearing . . .

I almost fell coming off the steps, avoided disaster by a slim margin, and plunged across the living room. I reached the kitchen in time to hear the outer sun porch door slam behind him: a flat, solid, final sound.

Bones in a forest clearing . . . white bones lying in white snow . . .

I didn't stop for my gloves, boots, or coat.

A horse's bones, a skeleton . . . picked clean . . .

I ran across the kitchen, striking a chair with my hip and knocking it over in my wake.

Toby's bones, Toby's skeleton . . . picked clean . . .

I crossed the sun porch in three long strides, bounding like an antelope.

Picked clean . . .

I tore open the door and went out into the black and snow-filled night.

Bones . . .

"Toby!"

The cold slammed into me and rocked me badly, as if sharp icicles had been thrust deep into my joints, between muscle and sheath, through arteries and veins. That was the "one" of a one-two punch that Nature had for me. The "two" was the wind which was seething up the hill at better than fifty miles an hour: a mallet to drive the icicles deeper.

"Toby!"

No answer.

For four or five or six seconds, as I desperately searched the bleak night ahead, I couldn't see him. Then suddenly I got a glimpse of his bright red pajamas outlined against the snow and flapping like a flag in the wind.

"Toby, stop!"

He didn't obey, of course. And now he was nearly out of sight, for visibility was just about nil.

Bones . . .

In the knee-deep snow—which was more likely hip-deep for him—I was able to make much better time than he did. Within a few seconds I reached him and caught him by the shoulder and pulled him around.

He struck me in the face with one small fist.

Surprised more than hurt by the blow, I tumbled backwards into a drift.

He pulled loose and turned and started down toward the woods once more.

Hundreds of big bear traps began to go off all around me: *snapsnapsnapsnapsnapsnapsnap!* And then I realized that I was only hearing my teeth chattering. I was half-frozen although I had spent no more than a minute in these sub-zero temperatures, lashed by this ferocious wind. Toby would have to be in even worse shape than I was, for his cotton pajamas offered less protection from the elements than did my jeans and thick flannel hunting shirt.

I pushed up and went after him, weaving like a drunkard in anxious pursuit of a rolling wine bottle. In a dozen steps I caught Toby by the shoulder and stopped him and pulled him all the way around.

He swung at me a second time.

I ducked the blow.

As he pulled back to swing again, gazing through me with lifeless eyes, I threw both arms around him and lifted him off the ground.

He kicked me in the stomach.

The breath rushed out of me like air exploding from a pin-pricked balloon. I lost my balance, and we both collapsed in a heap.

He pulled loose and scrambled away.

I went after him on my hands and knees, which felt like four blocks of ice. I saw him, closed the gap, lunged, and brought him down with a tackle. I rolled with him, holding him close, holding him tightly so that he couldn't get hurt—and so he couldn't kick and punch.

He bit me.

Hard.

But that was all right with me because I pretty much had been expecting it and had steeled myself against both the pain and the surprise of it. As he chewed viciously at my shoulder, surely drawing blood but making no sound whatsoever, I clambered laboriously to my feet, still holding on to him.

A thin crust of snow had frozen in my eyelashes, welding them into a pair of brittle plates. Every time I blinked it felt as if two heavy wooden shutters were crashing into place. Furthermore, my face was numb, and my lips felt as if they had cracked and were bleeding.

I took several uncertain steps through the soft drifts until I grasped that I was moving downhill rather than up—and thus away from the farmhouse. I searched for the house, for the light in the living room—and saw, instead, a dozen or more radiant eyes, amber eyes, glowing at me from thirty yards away, strange circles of warm light that pulsed like beacons through the blizzard. Crying out involuntarily, I whirled and ran uphill as fast as I could lift and put down my ice-caked legs.

Toby squirmed against me, stopped biting, tried to use his knees and elbows to injure me. But I was holding him too tightly for him to get any leverage.

A familiar pressure bloomed suddenly around my head, sought entrance, quickly found a way in to me, and danced over the surface of my brain . . .

No!

I resisted the contact.

Bones . . . think of bones . . .

I picked up speed.

Fear welled up in me as the pressure increased inside my skull; and it was a hideously potent fear, that biological terror that had made a raging madman of me in the forest earlier in the day. But I couldn't afford to lose my wits now. If I began to run blindly in circles, shouting and throwing punches at the empty air, the aliens would capture Toby and me; and before long they would go into the house and get Connie as well. Now that they had attempted to steal Toby from us, I was prepared to give serious consideration to that melodramatic and trite science fiction concept which I previously had found, if not impossible, highly improbable: that they viewed us as nothing more than a rich and convenient source of protein. Our survival, therefore, might well depend upon two things: how successfully I could resist the insistent mental probes—and how successfully I could cope with the disabling fear, the shattering terror, which the probes sparked in me.

Toby continued to struggle.

Clutching him against my chest, I managed to keep going.

The alien tried to sink thought-fingers into my mind, but I pinched and jabbed and scratched at his mental front, resisted and resisted and resisted.

Mindless fear slammed at me like hurricane seas, like gigantic waves battering a seawall. I held against them.

I kept running.

Lights were switched on ahead of me.

I could see the house, the sun porch.

Fifty feet. Maybe less.

I was winning.

Then I fell.

Still holding Toby—who had quieted considerably over the last few seconds—I sat up in the snow and looked down the hill toward the forest. The amber eyes were closer than they had been only half a minute ago, no more than thirty or thirty-five feet away from us now.

Images formed behind my eyes, fragments of light and brilliant colors, alien scenes . . .

No! Stay out of me!

Fear . . . crushing fear . . . terror . . . things in my head . . . spiders in my skull, things eating away in my brain . . .

I had to fight it and I did fight it and I was nonetheless sure that I was losing where I had been winning an instant ago.

I started to get up. My feet slipped out from under me. I fell again and saw that the amber eyes were even closer, twenty feet away and moving rapidly in on me, and I saw that I was not going to get away and I started to cry and —

—and then Connie appeared beside me, stepping

85

like a stage actress through the snow curtain. She was carrying the pistol that I had left at the head of the stairs. She was wearing a coat over her night gown, and her long hair was matted with snow that was crystalizing into ice. Bracing herself against the wind, holding the pistol with both hands, she fired at the approaching creatures.

The wind swallowed most of the sound of the shot.

Although none of the aliens appeared to have been wounded, they seemed to realize that they were being fired upon, and they seemed to view the pistol as a very real danger. After she got off her second shot—again hitting nothing—they stopped where they were and stared at us with those huge, unblinking eyes. Apparently, there was at least one blessing for which we could be grateful: these things were evidently not all-powerful, not invincible and unstoppable, as years of horror movies had conditioned me to think they would be.

The pressure abruptly evaporated in my skull. The mental probes were discontinued.

Squinting, I tried to see what sort of beings lay behind the amber eyes—however, the darkness and the snow defeated me. For all that I could tell, they consisted only of eyes, great disembodied discs of light adrift on the wind.

Shouting in order to be heard above the storm, Connie said, "Are you all right?"

"Good enough!" I shouted back at her.

"Toby?"

"He's okay, I think."

I got up.

The aliens stayed where they were.

"Do you want the gun?" she asked.

"You keep it," I said. "Let's get moving. But don't turn your back on them."

I was half-frozen. My muscles felt as if they were on fire although the flames were icy, and my joints were arthritic from the fierce cold. Each step was a miracle and an agony.

As if we were playing a child's game, we backed slowly toward the farmhouse. We kept our eyes on the alien eyes, and we tested the treacherous ground behind us before committing ourselves to each step. Gradually, a gap opened between us and our other-worldly visitors. We stepped into the square of wan light that spilled out through the sun porch windows —and in no more than two minutes we were safely inside.

"Lock the door," I told her.

"Don't worry about that."

I carried Toby into the kitchen and put him on the table while she bolted the sun porch door as well as the door that connected the porch to the kitchen.

"Did they come after us?" I asked, wondering if they were now pressing against the sun porch's glass walls.

"I didn't see them. I don't think they did."

The house was warm, but we suddenly felt colder than we had when we'd been out in the storm. It was the contrast, I suppose. We began to shake, twitch, and shiver.

"We have to get Toby out of those pajamas," Connie said, hurrying out of the room. "I'll get a fresh pair for him—and some towels."

Toby appeared to be asleep. I touched his wrist and counted his pulse. The beat was steady, neither too fast nor too slow.

A moment later Connie returned with clean pajamas and a huge stack of towels. I dried my hair while she attended to Toby. As she wrestled him out of his soaked, frozen pajamas, she said, "He's bleeding."

"It's okay," I said, my voice quivering with a chill.

"There's blood around his mouth," she insisted.

"It's my blood, not his."

When she had him free of his pajamas and wrapped in two big bath towels, she wiped his face and saw that what I said was true. *"Your* blood?"

"They took control of his mind," I said, recalling the nightmare battle in the snow. "And they made him bite me when he was trying to get loose and go to them."

"My God!"

"They almost had him."

She swayed.

I went to her and took the towel out of her hand. "Get your coat off. Dry your hair. You'll catch pneumonia standing around like that." I began to dry Toby's hair. I was staying on my feet only by dogged determination. I tasted my own blood: my lips had split from the cold, and now they burned and itched.

She said, "Are you all right?"

"Just cold."

"The bite?"

"It's not much."

"Your lips—"

"That's not much either."

Staring down at Toby, putting one slender hand against his face, she said, "Is he just unconscious?"

"Get out of the coat and dry your hair," I told her again. "You'll catch your death."

"Is he just unconscious?"

"I don't know."

"He'll be all right, won't he?"

"I don't know."

She glared at me, her pretty jaw suddenly set as firm as if it had been cast in concrete. She was wild-eyed, her delicate nostrils flared. She raised her hands: they were curled into small fists. "But you *must* know!"

"Connie—"

"When they took control of him—did they shatter his mind in the process?"

I finished drying his hair, tried not to look at her, tried not to think about what she had said, which was what I had been saying to myself for the last couple of minutes.

She was determined to get an answer out of me. "Is he just a vegetable now? Is that at all possible? Is that what they've done to him?"

As my hands warmed up they began to itch and go numb on me. The towel slipped out of my hands.

"Is it?" she demanded.

Toby said, "Mom? Dad?"

She grabbed the edge of the table.

I helped him sit up.

Blinking like a man stepping out of a cellar into sunlight, Toby looked at me, looked at her, coughed gently, shook his head, smiled tentatively, and said, "What . . . what the heck happened? I feel so . . . awful cold. Can I have some hot chocolate?"

Connie embraced him and started to cry.

Feeling hot tears swelling up at the corners of my own eyes, I went across the room to the cupboards to find mugs, spoons, and the big tin of cocoa mix.

FRIDAY

The Neighbors

10.

We had to get help. We had to let someone in the outside world know what was happening at Timberlake Farm.

Until now I had thought that we would be most well off if we remained as calm as we possibly could and stayed right where we were and waited out the storm. In time the telephone service would be restored, and we could call the sheriff in Barley to ask for help. But now I saw that, with the second snowstorm coming so fast on the heels of the first one, the phone might be out of order for three, four, or five days, even longer. By the time the lines were finally repaired, we would all have gone the way of Blueberry and Kate . . . When the telephone next rang—there would not be anyone alive to answer it.

The ideal solution was evident if impractical: we would all get dressed in our warmest clothes, put on our snowshoes, and walk out of here when dawn came a few hours from now. Just walk off, bold as you please. Just stroll out through the open fields, over the hills, on through another stretch of woods but not the same woods in which the aliens had landed, straightaway to the Johnsons' farm where we could call the sheriff on their telephone (which was an altogether different line from ours) and get help

. . . It was a pleasant fantasy—but it was a long way from reality. The Johnsons, our nearest neighbors, lived slightly more than two miles from Timberlake Farm. Although Toby was very self-sufficient, he was still a child with a child's limited physical stamina. In this brutal weather he could never hike two miles on snowshoes, probably not even one mile. And neither Connie nor I would come through alive if we had to take turns carrying him; the burden would sap us and leave us floundering weakly in deep drifts. As with everything else in this life, the ideal was unattainable and even laughable; therefore, I would have to seek help on my own and leave the two of them behind—leave them alone in the farmhouse.

Once we had made that decision—Connie and I sitting in easy chairs in the living room, Toby sleeping on the sofa in front of us—we had to choose between two courses of action. I could try to get help in Barley. Or I could hike to the Johnson farm and plead my case there.

First of all: Barley. I could walk due east, along our private lane, until I reached the county road that lay a bit less than two miles from here. The first time that a snowplow came along, I could flag it down and ride in to Barley. It appeared to be a simple plan, nearly fool-proof. But there might be complications. What if there were no snowplows working the county road—no traffic moving whatsoever? After all, it was not a main route. It served a handful of rural families who *expected* to be snowbound for weeks every winter and who would not ordinarily be bothered if the road remained closed for several days. In a blizzard of these dimensions, the county and state highway maintenance crews might concentrate their efforts in the towns and on the superhighways and primary

94

state routes that were more heavily used. With the wind drifting shut highways they had plowed open hours earlier, they would be kept busy with the major thoroughfares—while I might stand beside the county road for hours, waiting in vain and gradually freezing to death. If no plows came by I would have to return to the farmhouse in defeat—or walk yet another two miles to the nearest house that fronted on the county road, without any guarantee that when I got there I would find someone at home and/or a working telephone.

"If you went in that direction," Connie said thoughtfully, "I don't believe you'd find help in time. I don't think you'd make it through to Barley."

"Neither do I."

"Then we rule it out?"

"Yeah." Both of us had changed into dry clothes and had drunk mugs of steaming cocoa. I closed my eyes, wishing that I could hold on to the warmth of the house and not have to go outside again. "So I'll have to go to the Johnson farm."

"We always say it's two miles from here. But is that right?"

"That's what Ed told us."

"Two miles . . . But two miles as you walk—or two miles as the crow flies?"

That was a disturbing thought. I had never walked the full route any farther than to the top of Pastor's Hill from which you could look out across a forest and see the Johnson farm perched on another hill in the distance. I opened my eyes and said, "If it's as the crow flies, it could be considerably more than two miles on foot. Might be three or four miles. Might be too far for me."

She said nothing.

She stared at me with those incredibly beautiful eyes, bright gazelle eyes.

"But that has to be wrong," I said, trying hard to convince myself. "Look, when you tell someone that your nearest neighbor lives two miles away, you mean it's a two-mile walk or a two-mile drive—not a two-mile *flight*."

"Yeah, I guess that makes sense. But what if you get there and discover they aren't home?"

"They're homebodies. They'll be there."

"But just what if?"

"I'll break in and use their phone."

"And if the phone isn't working?"

"Then we're no better off than we were before I went—but we haven't lost anything by trying."

"You're right."

"And I'm positive they *will* be there."

"I remember . . . Ed has a gun case. Shotguns and rifles."

"Of course," I said, starting to feel better. "Every farmer around here goes hunting. So . . . Ed and I can arm ourselves . . . And even if the telephone lines are down at his place, we can come back here for you and Toby."

She sat up straighter, sat on the edge of her chair. "You know, I'm beginning to think maybe there's a chance."

"Sure. Sure, there's a chance. A *good* chance!"

"When will you leave?"

"At first light."

"That's only a few hours away. You'll need to get some sleep before you go," she said. "I'll sit up with Toby."

"You need to sleep too."

She grimaced. "We can't both sleep, that's for sure.

96

Besides, I've already slept for an hour, before Toby tried to run out on us."

"You can't get through tomorrow on one hour of sleep."

"And you can't hike to the Johnson farm without any sleep at all," she said, getting to her feet.

Realizing that she was right and I was a fool to argue, I folded up my misguided chivalry and tucked it away in a mental closet where it wouldn't attract me again. I got up and stretched and said, "Okay. Better wake me around five."

She came to me.

I put my arms around her.

She put her lips against my throat.

Warmth, a heartbeat, hope.

*   *   *

She switched off the lamp, plunging the living room into darkness, and came to the front door where I was waiting in my heavy coat, scarf, gloves, toboggan cap, boots, and snowshoes.

"When will you get there?" she asked.

"In this wind, on snowshoes . . . Four hours."

"With a couple of hours to rest at the other end, maybe you'll get back here by three or four in the afternoon."

"Sooner, I hope."

"I hope so too."

I wanted to be able to see her, to drift for a minute in the bright pools of her eyes.

"I love you," she said.

"I love you too," I echoed dumbly, meaning it with all my soul, wishing that there were some clever phrase that would say it better. "I love you."

Two patches of blacker black in the blackness of the room, we embraced, kissed, clung to each other for several seconds, clung like drowners to a raft.

"Better get moving," she said at last.

"Yeah." As I reached for the doorknob, I had a frightening thought. I froze and said, "If they take control of Toby again, you won't be able to restrain him. I was barely able to manage him. What'll happen?"

"It's all right," she said. "I've already thought of that. When I feed him breakfast, I'll powder one of my sleeping tablets in his hot chocolate."

"That won't hurt him, will it?"

"They're not *that* strong. He'll sleep like a baby most of tomorrow. That's all."

"And you think—so long as he's drugged, they can't make use of him?" I asked.

"What do *you* think?"

"I don't know."

"It'll work."

"I guess it will."

"Well," she said, "whether it'll work or not, it's really the only thing I can do."

After I'd looked at it from every angle, I had to agree with her. "But be extremely careful, Connie. Watch him as closely as you would if he weren't drugged. If they take control of him, they could make him attack you."

"I'll be careful."

I listened quietly, until I heard Toby breathing deeply and smoothly: he was still sound asleep on the living room sofa.

I said, "Keep the pistol with you."

She said, "I won't let it out of my sight."

"Don't let it out of your *hand*."

"Okay."

"I'm serious."

"Okay."

"And keep the safety off."

"I will."

"I shouldn't leave you alone."

"And I should make you take the gun in case they come after you along the way."

"They won't."

"They might."

I fumbled for her, hugged her. "You're in much worse danger than I am. I shouldn't leave."

"If we stay here together," she said, "we die here together." Softly: "Better get moving before there's too much light out there."

I kissed her.

She opened the door for me.

Then: cold, snow, ice, wind.

11.

Dawn had come but only technically. The sun had risen behind the dense dark storm clouds, but night had not yet gone to bed. The sun lay on the cloud-shrouded horizon, and there was nothing more than a vague glimmer of light in the world.

Cloaked in darkness, but with sufficient dawn glow to keep me from wandering off in the wrong direction, I struck out from the farmhouse. I headed due west toward Pastor's Hill which rose beyond the open fields comprising that flank of Timberlake Farm.

I floundered, getting accustomed to my snowshoes, and walked atop a hip-deep, cold dry sea of snow.

I didn't know if there were any aliens nearby or if they were watching me. I *did* know, from having listened to the radio, that this was no world-wide invasion, for there had been no news reports of strange yellow-eyed creatures. Thus far the aliens *seemed* to be concentrated in the woods behind the farmhouse—although they might well be on all sides of us.

If they *were* on all sides of us, if I were being watched right this minute, then there wasn't much of a chance of my ever reaching the Johnson farm.

But that was negative thinking, and it smacked of more than a little paranoia. Paranoia led to despair

101

and a feeling of utter helplessness. That kind of attitude could end in paralysis, a condition that already had been half-brought on by the wind and the snow. Determined to think positive, I used the darkness and the wavelike drifts to mask my stealthy progress toward the open fields toward Pastor's Hill.

If the aliens were out there keeping a vigil, they would never see me.

Never.

Not in a million years.

I *had* to believe that.

As I walked straight into the wind, shoulders hunched and head tucked down, I began to realize that what we were enduring would make the perfect subject matter for a book: my second book. The thought so surprised me that for a moment I stopped, stood quite still, oblivious of the wind and snow and of the possibility that some of the yellow-eyed creatures might be lurking in the drifts nearby.

Another book?

My first book had been published while I was a patient in a mental institution. It had not been a book so much as a diary, a war diary which I had kept from my first day of basic training until they brought me home from Asia as a mental basket case. Apparently, the diary helped satisfy the nation's need to see firsthand and fully grasp the horror of the last war, for it had placed high on all of the best seller lists across the country. It made a great deal of money for everyone concerned and was well reviewed. The sales were certainly not hurt by the fact that the author was a quasi-catatonic living in the equivalent of a padded cell. Indeed, that had probably helped sales more than all the publisher's advertising. Perhaps I was—in the eyes of my readers—a metaphor for the United States; perhaps they saw that the country had been driven as crazy as I had been by the war. And perhaps they thought they could learn some lessons from my ordeal that would be useful in getting them—in getting the entire country—back on sound footing.

But there was no salvation in the diary. I'm certain that most of them were disappointed. How could they have looked to me for their salvation when I hadn't been able to save myself?

I learned two things in the war:

Death is real and final.
The world is a madhouse.

Perhaps that doesn't mean much to you.
But it broke me.

These two realizations, combined with my own deep sense of guilt and moral failure, drove me over the edge. And it was the eventual acceptance of these bitter lessons, finding a way to live with these two truths, which made it possible for me to regain a tolerable perspective and a semblance of sanity.

The key is that *I* went through that hell, and it was by the flames that my wounds were cauterized. My readers—as well-meaning as they might have been— were merely arm chair sufferers. They were anxious to pass through the flames *vicariously*—and that will never be enough to cauterize their psychic wounds.

When I was released from the sanitarium—against all predictions, against all expectations—when it was clear I had a good chance of leading a relatively normal life (although the possibility of a relapse was never ruled out), I consented to be interviewed by a few reporters. I was asked this question more than any other: "Will you write another book?" And my reply was always the same: "No." I am not a writer. Oh, I suppose I have some facility with prose, but I'm surely no master of it. Now and again I have an original insight, a thing or two that I want to say. And I'm not excessively clumsy at characterization nor *too* free with flowery metaphors and overextended similes. I know my English grammar as well as the next college graduate. But I simply am not capable of the day-to-day, day-in-day-out, sustained effort of creation. That takes more sensitivity than I have—and a greater madness as well. I say madness, for even the worst godawful hack must believe—even if he denies it to everyone and to himself—that what he does makes a difference, however minuscule, in the course of human events. It really does not. I'm sorry, but that's true. The world is only a madhouse. And who can reason with madmen? Who can organize an asylum? To one degree or another, the majority of men (and women) are lunatics: religious fanatics, political fanatics, racial fanatics. You can't argue with them, for you can't educate them unless they want to be educated. And, my friends, they don't want. And if you write, instead, as a challenge not to the masses but to the ages, if you feel that you are flinging the gauntlet in the face of Time, then you don't understand the second thing that I learned in the last war:

Death is real and final.
Death is not a release from suffering.
Death is not a blessing.
Death is not a mystery.
Death is not a solution.
Death is not a trip to heaven.
Or to hell.

Or to limbo.

Or to nirvana.

Or to (fill in your favorite paradise).

Death is not a oneness with Nature.

Or with God.

Or with the universe.

Death is not reincarnation.

Death does not just happen to other people.

Death is not just what the villain deserves.

Death is not just a novelist's device.

Death is not heroic.

Death is not just for the movies.

Death is not just a stage we go through.

Death is not mutable.

Death is not beatable.

Death is not cheatable.

Death is not a joke.

Death. Is. Real. And. Final.

Final.

Forever.

And that's it.

So what else is there for a man to do but live while he can? What else makes sense but grabbing all the love and joy that you can, while you can, and to hell with trying to change the unchangeable? To hell with a writer's conscience, his morals, his vision, and his mission.

Yet here I was thinking about a second book. And I knew that, should we all survive (or even if I survived alone), the story would be told. I would do the telling. The agony of creation would be endured.

But why?

Not to educate the masses, surely. You know where I stand on that issue.

And not to entertain. There are dozens of writers who are far more clever, much wittier, and much more entertaining than I could ever hope to be. I'm no good at inventing thrills and chills, perhaps because the very worst in life has happened to me and pales the product of my imagination (although I still read thrillers and enjoy them).

Why, then, this book?

I suppose because, in the war, my diary became an important outlet for me. It was an unspeaking counselor, a silent psychiatrist, a priest to whom I could confess, wail, scream, whisper, vomit out the torment. And now, if we survived the ordeal at Timberlake Farm, I could best cleanse my soul of the stain if I put the story down on paper.

And having written it, why not make a buck or two? More money would mean a better chance of enjoying life fully.

I am being dangerously frank. Decry my attitude if you wish. Feel superior. Be my guest. I have nothing to lose.

But now that's been said, I must also say that there was another reason why I felt driven toward the writing of a second book. As I stood there in the snow, I sensed that this story had a unique aspect which demanded that it be told—not for the benefit of other men, not for the ages, but for something larger and greater than the fame-wealth-acceptance that most writers seek, something altogether indefinable.

Did the story have to be told for *them*—for the aliens?

But that made no sense. So far as I could see, they thought of us as animals, protein, mindless creatures, meat on the hoof. Even if my book were published and a copy placed before them, they most likely would not realize that writing and the making of books were signs of an intelligent species. To them a book might be as unremarkable an object as a stone or a clod of earth, for they might have evolved telepathy before language, thus making language unnecessary. To them, written symbols might be inconceivable. After all, if our farmhouse—a four-walled geometric structure of some sophistication when compared to a rabbit warren or a bear's den—was no indication to them that we were specimens of an intelligent species with whom they ought to communicate, with whom they should make every effort to be understood rather than feared, then no book would catch their notice or be at all meaningful to them.

And yet I knew that I would write it. And knowing that much, having accepted it, I was able to get moving once more. I walked on toward Pastor's Hill, through wind and snow, feeling no better nor any worse for having made that decision. I was merely perplexed by it.

I crossed the open fields and climbed the wooded slope of Pastor's Hill without encountering a single living creature born of this world or any other. On the crown of the hill, buffeted by the wind that roared through the bare branches and between the stark trunks of the trees, I stopped to rest.

With one hand over my eyes in the manner of an Indian scout in an old movie, I searched to the west for the Johnson farm which lay atop a bald hill beyond this arm of the forest. I could not see the house or the red barn or even the hill itself. The day had brightened considerably, but the snow was falling thick and fast, whipped relentlessly by the wind; and I could see no farther than a hundred yards.

I sucked on the winter air and began to move

again. At the bottom of Pastor's Hill, I crossed a narrow, frozen creek. My snowshoes rattled noisily on the ironlike surface.

On the far side of the creek I was stopped by another thought: without a compass I was sure to become disoriented and hopelessly lost in the forest maze. Up to this point, I had known the terrain fairly well, but from here on it would be all new to me. Somehow I had to maintain a westward heading, without deviation, if I were to reach the Johnson farm. At first I didn't see how I could be positive I was on a proper course. The sun was hidden by dense clouds, its light so diffused that I couldn't simply rely on keeping it behind my back to assure my westward progress. And then I realized that until the sun rose higher the western horizon would be the darkest of the four. This section of the woods— mostly maple, birch, elm, oak, and only a very few scattered evergreens—had been denuded by the cycle of the seasons; therefore, I could see the lowering gray clouds and mark my course by walking toward the gloomiest part of the sky. Soon the sun would rise high enough so that no distinction between dark and light horizons would be possible, but the system should see me most of the way through the forest if I hurried in advance of the dawn.

I lumbered forward. The bulky snowshoes were considerably less useful to me here than they had been out in the open fields, for they kept getting snagged in brush, briars, and brambles that poked through the snow. Nevertheless, persevering, I made fairly good time.

And I was not molested. Apparently, I had escaped the farmhouse without being seen.

At 9:30 in the morning I came out of the trees

into a pasture below the Johnson farm. The land rose gently, like a woman's breast, with the farm perched prettily atop the hill. There was no movement in or around the house, nor were any lights burning. At least I was not able to see movement or light from where I stood, although I was too far away to be absolutely certain.

The hillside was a fantasy of scalloped drifts, some of them too soft to bear my weight even though the snowshoes distributed it over a large area. Time and again I sank to my hips in powdery snow and had to claw my way out, wasting precious energy and minutes. My greatest fear, just then, was of dropping into a drift that was higher than my head—in which case I might exhaust myself trying to escape, pass out and freeze to death there, entombed in the fresh snow.

I tried not to think about that and kept plodding upward. By 10:00 I gained the crest, having taken half an hour to make what would have been a three-minute walk on a snowless day. I crossed the lawn to the back porch, clambered up the steps and over the porch to the rear door of the house.

The door was standing open. Wide open. The unlighted kitchen lay beyond.

I wanted to turn and go home.

That was impossible.

I knocked on the door frame.

Only the wind answered me.

"Hey!"

Nothing.

"Hey, Ed!"

The wind.

"Molly?"

Silence.

Then I noticed that the door had been open for

so long that the snow had drifted through it and had piled up to a depth of eight or ten inches on the nearest kitchen tiles. Reluctantly, I went inside.

"Ed! Molly!"

Who was I kidding?

There was no one in the kitchen.

I went to the cellar door, opened it, and stared down into perfect velvety blackness. When I tried the light switch, there was no response. I closed the door, locked it, and listened for a moment to be sure that nothing stirred in the cellar.

Next, I went to the kitchen cabinets and searched through most of the drawers until I found a twelve-inch, razor-sharp butcher's knife. Holding it as if it were a dagger, raised and ready, I went from the kitchen into the downstairs hall.

The house was as cold as the winter world outside. My breath hung in clouds before me.

Just inside the hall archway I stopped, peeled up the ear flaps on my hunting cap, and listened closely. But there was still nothing to hear.

The living room contained entirely too much furniture, but it was cozy: pine bookcases, three over-stuffed easy chairs with white antimacassars, two footstools, two floorlamps, three other lamps, a magazine rack, a faded velveteen divan with carved mahogany arms, a rocking chair, a magnificent old grandfather clock which had run down and was no longer ticking, a television set and a radio on its own stand, occasional tables covered with knick-knacks, and a stone fireplace with a statuette-bedecked mantel. A thick ceramic mug half-full of frozen coffee and a half-eaten breakfast roll were on the table beside one of the arm chairs, and there was an open magazine lying on the footstool before the chair. It looked as if someone had gotten up to answer the door and had never returned.

The dining room was directly across the hall from the living room. It was also deserted. I even opened the closet: cardboard cartons sealed with masking tape, a few lightweight summer jackets, photograph albums shelved like books . . .

There was a noise behind me.

I turned as quickly as I could, too clumsy in the snowshoes.

The room was as it had been.

I sat down and took off my snowshoes.

Another noise: a mechanical clicking . . .

Or was I hearing things?

Cautiously, I crept to the dining room doorway, hesitated on the brink of it like a paratrooper at the penultimate moment, and then leapt into the hall.

Nothing.

All was quiet.

Had it been my imagination?

The only other room downstairs was the den. The door was closed. I put my ear against it, but there wasn't anything for me to hear. Of course, I had made so much noise coming into the house that I would have alerted any of the aliens if they had been here. I raised the dagger high, gave the door a solid kick that threw it inward, and charged through, prepared to slash at anything that might be waiting for me.

No one was there.

No thing was there.

I kept the dagger raised, ready.

I followed the main hallway to the front of the house, intending to go upstairs—and I found the front door lying on the floor of the foyer, the house open to the elements. Although the door was half-buried under a couple of feet of snow that had sifted inside, I could see that it had been broken into three or four large pieces, smashed apart and thrown into the foyer. Shuffling closer, I examined the hinges which were still attached to the frame. The steel had been bent out of shape. The hinge bolts had been snapped as if they were pencil lead.

Stepping outside onto the front porch, I looked to the left, over at the barn. There was nothing out of place over there. The fields in front of the house were white and peaceful. The forest loomed near on the right, but there were no yellow-eyed creatures peering from between the trees.

None that I could see.

I went back into the foyer and stood there for at least five minutes, perhaps ten, listening, waiting to hear that clicking noise I'd heard in the dining room. But the silence was deep and unbroken. I seemed to be alone.

Flexing my fingers around the hilt of the butcher's knife, I went upstairs.

Five doors opened off the second-floor hall, and four of them were closed. The fifth had been smashed from its hinges and was lying half in the room and half in the corridor.

"Who's there?" I called.

My voice echoed against the icy walls.

I looked down the steps. They were empty. The snow in the foyer bore no footprints except for my own. Nothing had tried to creep up behind me. Yet.

Death does not just happen to other people.

Death is not just for the movies.

This is like the war, exactly.

Death is not mutable.

112

Death is not heroic.
Death is final.
Death is real.
Get out fast.
Get out!

I took one step toward the broken door, then another and another and a fourth, stopping only when the floorboards creaked and startled me. I listened to the wind in the attic and thought of all those moldy H. P. Lovecraft stories that I'd read when I was a kid. An eternity later I managed to take another step, and an eternity after that I reached the ruined doorway to the master bedroom. There, I froze and waited for something to happen.

But nothing happened.

"Hey!"

I felt as if this was Hallowe'en night and I was a child in a graveyard, timidly searching for ghosts that I didn't believe in but which I fully expected to find.

I stepped into the doorway and hesitated and then took one more step into the room.

Violence had been done here. A rocking chair was on its side, one arm smashed. The vanity bench lay in the corner by the dresser, splintered as if someone had taken an axe to it. The dresser mirror had been shattered; and shards of silvered glass were all over the floor. The bureau was on its side, drawers spilling from it and clothes foaming from the drawers.

I found the skeleton on the far side of the canopied bed. It was a human skeleton, sprawled gracelessly on the floor. It leered up at me. It held not even an ounce of flesh. Small, fine-boned, it was obviously a woman's skeleton. The remains of Molly Johnson.

12.

The Johnson farm was as real as pain, and at the same time it was also a clairvoyant vision, a psychic-flash premonition of our own fate: a warning that there was no possible future but this one for Connie, Toby, and me. The gigantic face of Death lay beneath me, the obscene mouth opened wide; and I balanced precariously—in the style of bespectacled Harold Lloyd, but grimly, grimly—on the dark and rotting lips. I walked through the house, barn, and stable like a man moving, dazzled and amazed, through the jagged landscape of a demented, paranoid nightmare which was as solid and as undeniable as Fifth Avenue.

We were going to die.

All of us: Connie, Toby, me.

There was no escape.

I knew it. I *felt* it.

But I told myself that the future could be shaped by one's own thinking, and that I must abandon negative thinking and embrace all that was positive.

Nevertheless, struggling with a Peale imitation, I continued to sense a rapidly approaching disaster of truly terrifying proportions.

When I found nothing more of interest in the farmhouse (no new skeletons), I went downstairs and outside, across the porch, into the whirling snow.

Without benefit of snowshoes, I went to the barn, bulling my way through knee-deep snow and walking around the more formidable drifts.

The winter world was a kaleidoscope of death: rotate the lens for countless disturbing images:

—the storm sky: waxy, mottled gray-black, as still as if it had been painted on a fine-grain canvas: the skin of a corpse;

—the wind: cold, crisp, enervating: the breath of the long-dead multitudes;

—the forest: deep, Stygian, mysterious: home of Goethe's terror, *Der Erlkonig;*

—the unbiquitous snow: milk-pure, bride-white, hymeneal: the death shrouds, the smooth satin lining of a new casket, age-bleached bones . . .

The barn doors slid open on well oiled runners.

I entered with the wickedly sharp butcher's knife held out in front of me, although I sensed that the weapon was now quite worthless. The enemy had come, had taken all that was wanted, and had gone away from this place a long, while ago. The barn no longer contained any danger that could be dispatched with a well honed knife.

I stepped out of the cold winter wind into motionless air that was even more chilling.

The barn was a mausoleum that contained the skeletons of sixteen fully grown milk cows. Fifteen of them were lying in railed milking bays, their heads toward the outside barn walls, fleshless haunches poking out into the hay-strewn central aisle down which I walked. They seemed to have died and been stripped of their flesh in an instant, much too swiftly for them to have become sufficiently agitated to snap their restraining ropes which were still intact, looped

116

around skeletal necks. The sixteenth set of bones was piled in the center of the aisle, the head having fallen more than a yard from the neck vertebrae, one keyboard of ribs smashed into hundreds upon hundreds of splinters; and the empty eye sockets spoke without voice but with an eerie eloquence.

As I walked the length of the barn, I tried to imagine how the cows had been dealt with so suddenly—and *why* it had been done. I was no longer absolutely certain that the aliens had killed for food; indeed, the longer I thought about it the more foolish and small-minded that explanation seemed; and instead, it occurred to me that these creatures might have been taking specimens of earth's fauna. And yet . . . If that were the case, why wouldn't they want the bones along with everything else? Why wouldn't they take the whole animal as it had been in life? Perhaps they had been seeking neither food nor specimens. They might well have reasons that only they could ever understand, motivations that I (or any other man) would find incomprehensible.

It was craziness.

Of course: the world is a madhouse: most people are lunatics: the laws of the universe are irrational, insane: the other lesson from the last war.

I looked up at the lofts on both sides.

Nothing was looking back down at me.

At the other end of the barn, the big sliding door was all the way open. Snow and spicules of ice were sheeting inside. The bare skeleton of Garbo, Ed Johnson's German shepherd, made a graceless heap on the sill, lying both in and out of the building. The lupine skull had been shattered at the very top and then cracked into surprisingly even halves from brow to

117

tip of snout, as if the dog had suffered a sudden, brutally sharp blow with a length of iron pipe directly between and above the eyes. Its yellow-white teeth, as pointed as needles, appeared to be bared in a hideous snarl, but that was nothing more than the naked rictus common to any skull, whether human or animal, when it was revealed without the adornment of flesh.

If the aliens finally got to me, I would look exactly like that: grinning/snarling at eternity.

That's how Connie would look, too.

And Toby.

Premonitions . . .

I stepped over Garbo and walked outside where I found what remained of Ed Johnson. Just his bones, of course. His battered pickup truck stood twenty feet away, facing the barn door. A drift had built up all along the passenger's side, as high as the window and into the cargo bay. The driver's door was open, pressed back against the front fender by the steady wind; and a man's skeleton was crumpled in the snow beside the truck. Snow was drifted over parts of it and filled up the empty rib cage. One macabre arm was raised from the elbow, and the fingers appeared to be grasping the winter air.

In the stable that stood behind the barn and beyond the abandoned pickup truck, there were three horses as well as a cat that had been named Abracadabra (for the way it had made mice disappear from the house and barn within a week after it had taken up residence with the Johnsons): now four skeletons. While it was no less horrifying than my first encounter with the aliens hideous litter (poor Blueberry's bones in that forest clearing yesterday afternoon, discarded as a human camper might thoughtlessly discard the

118

be no yellow-eyed creatures from beyond the stars, where there would not be any trouble of any sort, where there would be nothing, nothing . . .

As frightened of these negative thoughts as I was of the aliens, I bent and scooped up handfuls of snow and pushed them in my face. I gasped and coughed and spluttered, recovered enough to stagger toward the farmhouse once more.

But what next?

Toby . . .

Connie . . .

How could I save them?

Or were they already dead?

And as before I thought:

The Johnson farm was a real pain, and at the same time it was also a clairvoyant vision, a psychic-flash premonition of our own fate: a warning that there was no possible future but this one for Connie, Toby, and me.

The gigantic face of Death lay beneath me, the obscene mouth opened wide; and I balanced precariously—in the style of bespectacled Harold Lloyd, but grimly, grimly—on the dark and rotting lips.

And my feet were slipping.

13.

In only five minutes I had a stack of logs burning in the big living room fireplace. They crackled, hissed, popped, and sent thin smoke up the stone flue. The flames were yellow-orange and danced wildly in the draft. Not surprisingly, the room looked about one thousand percent cheerier in the warm, flickering light.

Although I had no appetite, I went out to the kitchen to look for food. If I had to hike all the way back to Timberlake Farm after resting for only one hour, then I needed to eat something, pack in fuel to replace what I'd burned up getting here. Molly Johnson's pantry was well-stocked—however, most of the food had been ruined by the long deep freeze that had begun soon after the electric power had failed. Fruit, vegetables, and other goods that had been packaged in jars were now unedible, for they had frozen, expanded, and shattered the containers: shards of glass now prickled the frozen contents. Most of the cans were swollen and would have been the end of any can opener. I found a homemade chocolate cake in the bread box, however, and a half-gallon of vanilla ice cream in the refrigerator. I took the cake and the ice cream—both of which were like lumps of granite—to the fireplace to thaw them out a bit. Soon, the ice cream melted, and the cake grew soft. I managed to finish two respectable portions of each. Then I brought snow in from outside and melted it in a bowl. I drank the warm water which turned out to be the best part of the lunch and made me feel better than I had in hours.

(Why such a lengthy description of a meal that was something considerably less than a gastronomic delight? Because I don't want to get on with what remains of the story? Quit stalling, Hanlon. Put it down on paper, every last terrible twist and turn of it, down on paper and out of your system in the very best tradition of self-analysis. *Then* you can go quietly mad.)

In the den I examined all of the weapons in the gun case. I chose a rifle with telescopic sights and a double-barrel shotgun. I loaded both weapons and carried them to the living room along with two boxes of ammunition.

By this time I was extremely anxious to get going, for I did not like to think of Connie and Toby all alone at Timberlake Farm—especially not as the day rushed toward an early winter sunset. I also didn't like to think of trekking through the woods in the dark, easy prey for Nature and the aliens. Yet I understood that if I were to make another long journey in the snow, I would have to stay here before the fire for an hour or until my bones as well as my clothes were warm and dry. And as impatient as I was to get moving, I sat there as long as it took for the fire to revive me. In the dancing flames I saw faces: Connie, Toby, and a face composed solely of two enormous yellow eyes . . .

At one o'clock in the afternoon, I left the Johnson

farm by way of the same hill and pasture over which I'd come.

The rifle was strapped across my back.

I carried the shotgun in my right hand.

I was ready for anything.

At least I *thought* I was.

It was not easy going. And that's an understatement. The temperature had dropped fifteen or twenty degrees from where it had stood this morning and must now be hovering well below zero even without the wind chill factor figured into it. And the wind chill factor had to be considerable, for the wind was coming in from the west with the same forty-mile-an-hour punch that it had been throwing at us (except for occasional fifty-mile-an-hour gusts and sixty-mile-an-hour squalls) for nearly seventy-two hours. Furthermore, new drifts had built up everywhere, and many of them had not yet formed crusts thick enough to support my weight. I fell into them and struggled out and got to my feet and walked a few steps and fell again, pratfall after pratfall. It became monotonous. After what seemed like six or eight hours of grueling, Herculean effort, I came to a familiar limestone formation against which I had rested for a spell this morning when I had been traveling in the opposite direction. The limestone marked the halfway point through this arm of the forest, which meant that I was only one-quarter of the way back to Timberlake Farm. I allowed myself less than five minutes, then started out once more. I walked eastward, judging my direction by certain formations of land and trees and brush which I had carefully committed to memory on the way westward earlier in the day. The wind blew and the snow snowed and the cold chilled and the light gradually went out of the gray sky as if some celestial hand were slowly turning a rheostat switch up above the clouds.

* * *

I was lying on my back under a bare elm tree, resting. I had no idea how I had gotten there; I couldn't remember lying down. And I was lying on the rifle which was still strapped across my back. . . Odd. Distinctly odd. . . But much more comfortable than I would have thought. Oh yes. So comfortable. Just lovely. I felt warm and snug. I could look up through the interlacing black branches and watch the pretty little lacy snowflakes spiraling down to the earth. So very pretty and warm and soft and pretty and soft and warm, warm, warm, warm. . .

Hanlon, don't be a fool, I told myself.

Well I like it here, I answered.

For eternity?

Five minutes will do.

Eternity.

Will you stop messing in my comfortable world?

Get up.

No.

Get up!

I rolled onto my side, sat up, clutched at the trunk of the tree, and got my numbed feet under me again. My sense of balance was functioning about as well as it would have done had I just now stepped off the biggest, fastest roller coaster in the world. The world circled around and around me. . . Nevertheless, I got going once more, head down and thrust out in front of me, teeth clenched and jaws bulging, shotgun in one hand, the other hand fisted, looking and feeling mean as a treed raccoon.

126

* * *

A clump of powdery white stuff fell out of the laden pine boughs overhead and struck me in the face. I spluttered, coughed, cursed, groped around in the snow, found the shotgun just inches from my fingers, used it as a staff, and levered myself to my feet.

I thought smugly, How about *that* for stamina? Huh? Now that is what you call true grit.

But right away the pessimistic half of me leaped into the conversation with both mental feet. If that snow, I said sternly to myself, hadn't fallen smack in the middle of your ugly face, you know where you would still be? You would still be right there on the ground, under that tree; you'd be there until you finally froze to death.

Not true!

Sure is.

I was resting.

Resting?

Conserving strength.

Well, every minute you spend "conserving strength" is one more minute that Connie and Toby—remember them, Connie and Toby, wife and son?—spend all alone in the farmhouse.

Hey, you really know how to spoil a good mood, don't you?

Yeah.

I guess I've rested enough.

You better believe it.

Determined to put an abrupt end to this interminable interior dialogue, I oriented myself, took a deep breath of air that seemed instantly to crystallize my lungs, and walked westward. Within a few minutes I came to a narrow frozen creek. I crossed it and went up the western slope of Pastor's Hill.

On the crest I braced myself against the wind that pummeled my back, and I stared out at the open fields of Timberlake Farm. The house was concealed by billowing curtains of snow. But it was out there, just beyond my sight, and I would be home in an hour or so. Just one more mile to go, the last mile, the easiest mile by far, right across open land, no trees or hills or briars or brambles, easy, simple, sweet, a real cakewalk.

*　　*　　*

Darkness.
Softness.
Warmth.
And I kept thinking:
Death is not beatable.
Death is not cheatable.
Death is not mutable.
Death is real and final.
"I'm not dead yet!" I croaked, staggering to my feet.

I walked perhaps ten yards before I realized that I no longer had the shotgun; and I turned right around and went back to look for it. I passed the place where I had collapsed, kept going. Twenty or thirty feet farther on, I found the gun. The snow had nearly buried it. The black, ice-sheathed barrel poked up out of a drift just far enough to catch my eye. I pulled the weapon free, gripped it firmly in both trembling hands, and stomped off toward the house that was still shrouded in a shifting haze of snow.

Each step was agony. Pain shot up my legs, burned along my back. Only my feet were free of pain, for they were numbed by the intense cold.

I had trouble getting my breath.

I cursed my weaknesses as I walked.

(I am expending too much time and too many words recounting this journey back from the Johnson farm. And I know why I'm doing that; I can see through myself so easily. There are two reasons. One: I don't want to have to write about what follows this standard scene of wilderness survival. I don't want to face up to the memory. Two: I am trying with all my might to convince myself that I did everything I possibly could have done, everything any human being could have done. I walked for four miles through a furious storm, seeking help. Was it my fault that there was no help available at the other end? Stop stalling, Hanlon. Will you just get on with it?)

Darkness moved across the sky like spilled ink seeping through a carpet.

The temperature dropped.

Night came in full, squeezed tight around me, exciting claustrophobic fears.

I proceeded blindly, squinting at nothing, blinking away the tears that the cold wind had pressed from my eyes and which it now turned to ice on my cheeks. I kept moving, trusting to instinct to keep me headed for home, because I was terrified that the moment I stopped I would become confused, disoriented, and would wander helplessly in circles thereafter.

Snow: crusting in the eyelids, tickling in the nostrils, stinging the lips, melting on the tongue . . .

Wind: behind like a pursuing demon, pushing, shoving, battering, whistling against muffled ears . . .

I fell.

I got up.

I walked.

There was nothing else I could do.

How far to go?

Quarter of a mile.

How can you be sure?

Maybe half a mile.

I can't make half a mile.

Then it's an eighth of a mile.

I fell.

I didn't get up.

Darkness . . . warmth . . . softness like cotton blankets . . . a cup of warm cocoa . . . happiness . . .

As the vision drew me in, fear suddenly exploded and blew the image to pieces. I got up, licking my lips. I started walking, wondered if I were still going eastward, kept going.

I fell again.

I got up as far as my hands and knees, my head hanging down—and I realized that I was kneeling in a circle of pale yellow light. A shudder passed through me as I pictured half a dozen yellow-eyed creatures closing in around me, casting an eerie luminous glow before them. But I looked up and found that the light was coming from one of the farmhouse windows not more than ten feet away.

A minute later I fell against the front door, pounded on it, called for Connie, wept.

The door opened.

"Don!"

I stumbled inside, leaned against her when she offered a shoulder, and said, disbelievingly: "I'm home."

SATURDAY
12:00—1:00 A.M.

The Attack

14.

I didn't see it, of course. I cannot *know*. I can't retell it with perfect confidence in the tale. Nevertheless, it must have happened something like this:

A small herd of deer was sheltered in the forest where the snow didn't drift to such heights as it reached out in the open fields. They fed on the tough but juicy leaves of winter brush, on crow's foot and holly, on cold weather berries, of various sorts, on tender bark, and on those mushrooms that had survived far enough into the autumn to be quick-frozen by a sudden change in the seasons.

One buck fed at the edge of the herd. He nibbled on strips of peeling birch bark.

The wind was high above the trees, a distant howling like wolves held at bay by mounted hunters.

Now and again one of the deer would look up into the darkness overhead, never with fear but with curiosity.

The pine boughs—for this part of the forest was mostly pines—protected the deer from the worst of the storm.

The alien moved noiselessly through the trees.

The buck paused in his meal.

The alien came closer.

The buck stopped chewing, blew steam, drew

breath, tilted his magnificent head, listened, snorted, went back to the birch bark.

The alien closed in on him.

Suddenly aware of the foul odor of ammonia, the buck finally raised its proud head. It sniffed and shook its antlers and let a half-chewed mouthful of bark drop to the ground.

Some of the other deer turned to watch it.

The buck sniffed again.

By now all twenty-odd members of the herd had caught the ripe scent. None of them were interested in food any longer. They were motionless, except for their long eye lashes which trembled and except for their nostrils which, beaded with moisture, also trembled. They were waiting for the worst, hearts racing, ears pricked up. . .

The alien stopped ten yards away.

Snowflakes melted on the buck's nose.

The wind moaned. It seemed a bit louder than it had been a moment ago.

The buck stood very still for a while—until it saw the huge yellow eyes that were fixed on it. It froze for an instant, then panicked.

The alien moved in quickly.

The buck snorted and reared up on its hind legs——and the alien reached out and took full control of the simple animal mind.

One of the does squealed.

Then another: contagion.

The herd thundered away down the forest trail, white tails puffed up behind them, their hoofbeats silenced by the blanket of snow that misted up around them.

Only the buck remained.

The alien came out from the deep brush, shoving aside the jagged brambles and blackberry vines, snow pluming up from its many legs. It stepped onto the narrow path between the pines and approached the deer.

The buck blinked, quivered.

The other being immediately soothed it. Standing before the animal, the alien carefully examined it for all of half a minute, as if learning the uses of the beast, then turned away and lumbered down the trail in the direction that the herd had gone.

Head lowered, large brown eyes wide, the buck followed without hesitation. Its tongue lolled between its lips. Its tail was tucked down now: brilliant white side concealed, dull gray-brown side revealed.

The two creatures eventually left the woods and came out on a long slope where five other yellow-eyed beings were waiting for them.

The buck snorted when it saw the others.

Its heart thundered, threatened to burst.

The alien responded quickly, stilled the terror, slowed the heart—and kept rigid control.

Silently, they climbed the hill.

The buck was forced to jump through a number of deep drifts that nearly proved too much for it. It kicked and heaved. Its thick haunch and shoulder muscles bunched painfully. Steam spurted from its black nostrils.

Steam rose, too, from the broad, dark, slanted, shiny backs of the six aliens.

Shortly, a house came into sight atop the hill.

A farmhouse.

Timberlake Farm.

The attack had begun.

I took a quick, hot shower, sluicing away some of the chill which had curled like a segmented worm of ice deep inside of me. The worm had anchored itself with a thousand tendrils and could not be entirely torn loose. When I came out of the shower, I discovered that Connie had left a double shot of whiskey, neat, in a squat glass tumbler on the edge of the sink. I sipped at the first shot while I toweled off and dressed. Just before I went downstairs, I finished the second shot in one fiery gulp that scorched my throat and made my eyes water.

However, not even the whiskey—although it brought a bright flush to my face—could burn out every segment of the ice worm.

Connie and Toby were in the kitchen. They had both eaten earlier, but she was re-heating some homemade vegetable soup for me. Toby was sitting at the table, intently studying a large, half-completed jigsaw puzzle; I winced when I saw that it was a snow scene.

Even a stranger, stepping into that room without knowing anything about our situation, could have seen that we were living under siege conditions. The curtains had been drawn tightly over the window, and the sun porch door was closed, locked, and chained. The rifle lay on a chair near the table, and the loaded pistol was beside the water glass at the place Connie had set for me. But most of all there was an air of expectancy, a thinly masked tension in all of us.

I sat down, and she put a bowl of soup before me. I drew a deep breath of the fragrant steam and sighed. I had not been very hungry until the food was before me; and now I was ravenous.

While I ate Connie dried, dismantled, and oiled the shotgun which had taken a beating in the blizzard.

Toby looked up from his puzzle and said, "Hey, Dad, you know what happened?"

"Tell me."

"Mom put a spell on me."

"A spell?"

"Yeah."

I looked at Connie. She was trying to suppress a smile, but she didn't glance up from the shotgun on which she was working. I asked Toby: "What sort of spell?"

"She made me sleep all day," he said.

"Is that so. After you slept all the night before?"

"Yeah. But you know what else?"

"What else?"

"I don't believe it was a spell at all."

Now Connie looked up from her gun.

I said, "It wasn't a spell?"

Toby shook his head: no. "I think she slipped me one of her sleeping capsules in my breakfast orange juice."

"Why, *Toby!*" Connie said.

"It's okay, Mom," he said. "I know why you did it. You thought as long as I was asleep the aliens couldn't get me to run away again. You made me sleep to protect me."

I started to laugh.

"Boy child," Connie said to him, "you're really too much for me. You know that?"

He grinned, blushed, and turned back to me. "You going to tell us some more about what all you found over at the Johnson farm?"

The only thing I had told them thus far was that the aliens had been there ahead of me and that Ed and Molly were dead.

Connie quickly said, "Let your father eat his dinner, Toby. He can tell us later."

When I'd finished three bowls of soup, I told them about the skeletons at the Johnson farm and about the dead bull lying in the generator shed. I tried to stay calm, tried to leave out most of the adjectives and adverbs, but now and then I let the tale become too vivid, so vivid that they recoiled slightly from me.

After I had finished Toby said, "Then I guess we have to hold them off all by ourselves. We can do it."

Connie said, "I'm not so sure of that, general."

She looked at me, crow's feet of worry around her lovely eyes. "What are we going to do?"

I had been doing a great deal of thinking about that. "Just one thing we can do. Get out of here."

"And go where?"

"East."

"The county road?"

"That's right."

"You think it's been plowed open?"

"No."

She screwed up her lovely face. "Then you intend to walk to the nearest house?"

"We're all going to walk to the nearest house," I said. "The big white frame place in toward Barley."

"That house is four miles from here."

"I know."

"We already discussed that possibility—"

"We did?" Toby asked.

"Last night," she told him patiently, "when you were sleeping on the couch."

"I miss the interesting stuff," he said.

She said to me: "Toby can't walk four miles on snowshoes in this weather."

"I'm tough," he said.

"I know you are," she said. "But this is a blizzard. You aren't that tough."

The hall clock struck midnight.

Toby thought about it as the chimes rang, then nodded in agreement. "Well, yeah... Maybe I'm not quite *that* tough. But almost."

"And we can't carry him," she reminded me. "Neither one of us has had enough sleep. And after your trek to the Johnson farm... We'd never get through alive if we had to carry him."

"He'll walk as far as he can, and then we'll carry him the rest of the way," I said. "We don't have any choice. If we stay here we'll end up like Ed and Molly."

"Hey," Toby said, "you won't have to carry me. I can ride on a sled!"

16.

While Connie and Toby and I talked about escape, there was movement outside, the first stages of the attack.

The continuation of that unhuman scene:

There was no light other than the vague, pearly phosphorescence of the deep snow fields, a ghostly glow like the skin of an albino in a dark room.

Snow and tiny granules of ice sheeted on the wind.

Drifts rose to dunelike peaks.

(Von Daniken, visionary or true crazy, would certainly have appreciated the other element of this special night: six yellow-eyed gods—or devils—although the look of them would have blown most of his theories into dust. Somehow the gods who are supposed to have driven von Daniken's "chariots" all come off as very Nordic types, blond and handsome and clear-eyed and obviously cut out for movie stardom; but in reality, the universe does not repeat its own designs, and it has a few insane jokes up its sleeve as well. . .)

Five of the aliens stopped on the brow of the hill, just thirty yards from the farmhouse. They studied the door of the sun porch, studied the curtained kitchen window, studied the bright lamps that burned behind the living room windows. . .

Snow fell on them—however, it did not melt from their flesh as quickly as it would have melted from human skin. Indeed, the snow clung to them as it would have clung to fence posts or rocks or any cool, inanimate objects. A thin layer of snow sheathed them and quickly formed into a brittle crust. The crust turned to ice before it finally and gradually slid away in delicate, thin, transparent sheets—to be replaced by a new crust of snow that was still in the process of turning to ice.

Nevertheless, the steam rose from the pores on their broad and shiny backs.

The sixth creature stalked off toward the stable, away from its companions.

The buck followed the lone alien. It leaped out of a four-foot drift and fell into even deeper snow. It heaved and it twisted, its eyes bulging with the effort that it had to expend to free itself.

The alien turned and stared.

The buck struggled.

The alien calmed it, made it more purposeful.

The buck broke loose, wheezing.

The alien continued toward the stable. At the stable door it stopped again, slipped the bolt, pushed the door open, and quickly stepped out of the way.

The buck toddled forward, unsteady, not unlike a fawn first finding its legs.

The alien allowed it to rest for a moment, then gave it new purpose.

Having regained some of its strength, the buck entered the building in much the same sort of trance that had afflicted poor Blueberry when she had walked out of there on her way to becoming a pile of bones.

There were no lights inside the barn. And only

one rather small window admitted the minuscule light of the snow fields.

This did not seem to bother the buck. Its eyes had been designed to insure survival when the big northern wolves prowled by night.

The alien—amber eyes aglow, emitting some light of their own—was not disturbed by the darkness either. It watched the buck through the open door.

There was no wind in the barn, but the long gallery was cold, for the electric heaters had been switched off over twenty-four hours ago.

The buck sniffed the dead air—and sensed the body of the horse that lay within one of the stalls on the right-hand side. Its tightly controlled mind turned over like a sick stomach, and rebellion flickered in it.

The alien clamped down hard.

The buck staggered sideways, stumbled, and fell onto its forelegs, bleating in pain.

The alien waited.

The buck was still.

At last the alien eased up on the mental reins.

The buck knelt where it was, dazed.

The alien gave it instructions: quick, silent pulses of thought.

The animal got its forelegs under it again, and it walked down the stable row.

To the generator.

It sniffed.

The generator hummed.

The buck backed up a few feet and lowered its antlers.

17

"A sled?" Connie asked.

"My Red Runner out on the sun porch," Toby said.

She took hold of his hand and gently squeezed it. "That's good thinking, honey." Then she looked at me and said, "That would work, wouldn't it? A sled?"

Toby was excited and pleased with himself. "I could walk *some* of the way. Maybe a whole mile. And then when I just couldn't walk one step more, you could take turns pulling my sled until I got rested up real good. That wouldn't be so hard as carrying me. Hey, Dad? What do you think?"

"The runners are going to sink through the drifts and get bogged down," I said.

Toby said, "Bet they won't."

"They will," I assured him. "But that doesn't mean that your idea is a bad one. A sled's the perfect answer. We just have to use the right *kind* of sled— one without runners."

"Without runners?" Toby said.

"A length of heavy plastic with ropes tied to it. You could lie down on the plastic, flat out on your belly, spreading your weight over a larger area than a pair of runners. . ."

"Great!" Toby said.

"You really think it'll work?" Connie asked.

"I really do."

"Fantastic!"

Connie leaned forward, propped her arms on the table, and said, "Where do we get a sheet of plastic?"

"We could use the bags that we get our clothes in from the dry cleaners," Toby suggested.

"No, no," I said. "That's much too thin. That would tear to pieces before we'd towed you a hundred feet."

"Oh, yeah." He frowned at his own suggestion and began to look around the room for a source of sturdy plastic.

I folded my hands around a coffee cup and thought and couldn't find a solution. I was tired and stiff and sore. I wanted to sleep.

After three or four minutes of silence, Connie said, "Does it have to be plastic?"

"I guess not."

"Wouldn't a length of heavy canvas do the job just as well?"

"Sure," I said.

"Well, all that stuff the owners have stored in the basement—it's all wrapped up in canvas tarps. We can unwrap something. If the tarp's too large, we can cut it down."

"Perfect," I said.

"Where will you get the rope?"

I thought a moment. Then: "Wire will be just as good as rope. There's a big roll of that down in the tool cabinet."

"When do we leave?"

"Now?" Toby asked.

"We'd get lost in the dark," I said.

146

"You didn't get lost when you came home in the dark from the Johnson's," he said.

"Dumb luck."

"I think you're great, Dad."

That compliment lifted my spirits higher than I can say. For the first time I realized that, because of this ordeal, I had the chance to prove myself to Toby, to erase his memories of the way I had looked in the hospital, much faster than I could have done without the current crisis. "Thank you," I said. "You're not too bad yourself, chief."

He grinned broadly, blushed brightly, and looked down at his jigsaw puzzle.

"Maybe by morning," Connie said, "the wind and the snow will have stopped."

"Maybe. But don't count on it. We'll leave at first light, and we'll expect the weather to be against us every step of the way."

"What about sleep?" Connie asked.

"I'm not sleepy," Toby said. "I slept last night, and then Mom doped me up this morning. I'm just getting awake."

"Well, you'll have to try to sleep anyway," I said. "When we start out tomorrow, you'll need to be refreshed." I turned to Connie, who, like me, had bags under her eyes. She'd had only one hour of sleep in the last thirty-six hours, and I had not had much more than that, perhaps three hours. We were both on the verge of collapse. "We'll sleep in shifts again," I told her. "You go first. I'll go down to the basement and see about the tarp."

"Can I come along?" Toby asked.

Getting up from the table, I said, "Sure. You've got to give me a hand with this job."

Connie got up, came into my arms, and hugged

147

me for a moment. Then she kissed my neck and stepped back, turned, started toward the living room arch.

"I'll wake you in three hours," I said.

She turned. "Sooner than that. You've had a rougher time of it than I have. Besides, you've always needed more sleep than me."

"Three hours, and don't argue," I said. "Go hurry up and sleep. Morning's coming too fast."

18.

This method has become compulsive: this careful step-by-step breakdown of that most crucial hour of my life, this prolonged narrative of events which certainly moved much more swiftly than this in real life. (Yes, in fact it had all happened much too fast.) But there is no other way that I can tell it, obsessed with it as I am, ruled by it as I am, broken and destroyed by it as I am. . . Once more, therefore, let the imagination flow, look outside the farmhouse and return to the barn where the alien now stands at the open door looking inside:

The buck lowered its antlers. It snorted and pawed at the earthen floor much like a bull will stroke the arena as a warning to the matador.

The generator hummed.

The buck charged the machinery.

The collision was solid, brutal, and noisy: a loud, reverberating gong.

The buck rebounded. It fell backwards on its haunches and made a miserable noise.

The alien soothed the animal mind.

The buck rose. It shook its head.

The generator was still functioning.

The buck charged again. The gong sounded. A

*piece of the magnificent antlers broke off and fell on
top of the machinery.*

The generator hummed.

(If the aliens understood the purpose of the
generator—and it is clear that they must have understood it, for they knew exactly why it must be
destroyed—then why couldn't they grasp the fact
that we were members of an intelligent race and not
merely dumb beasts like the buck? Why? In all the
science fiction novels I read when I was a kid, the
aliens and the humans always recognized the intelligence in each other, no matter what physical differ-
ences they might have had. In those books the aliens
and the humans worked together to build better uni-
verses—or they fought each other for control of the
galaxies—or they struggled to at least live together
in mutual tolerance or— Well, why wasn't it like that
in real life, when the first beings from the stars met
the first men (us)? Well, that's easy to answer, Hanlon. They might have known what a generator was—
and yet not think of it as the product of a civilized
culture. To them it might seem unbelievably crude,
the symbol of a culture as primitive to them as apes
are to us. The generator, obviously, did not make
us worthy of their concern. And is that so difficult
to grasp? Don't the ants build elaborate cities, stage
trials of their "criminals", and *elect* queens? Hasn't
that been studied and recorded by hundreds of
entomologists? Sure. But we step on them all the
same, don't we? We crush them by the tens of thou-
sands with no thought given to their tiny civilization.)

*Turning to face the stable door, the buck put its
back to the machinery. It began to kick out like a
bronco, slamming its hooves into the metal housing
that protected the moving parts.*

150

The sheet steel bent.

The glass face of a gauge shattered.

Something went ping! like a ricocheting bullet.

The animal kicked out again.

The metal clanged! and buckled.

Another kick.

No effect.

And another.

Rivets popped.

Yet another.

A second gauge broke.

Hooves drummed on steel.

Yet the generator hummed.

The buck stopped kicking. It turned around, faced the purring machinery once more, lowered its head, and plowed straight into the two heavy, pine stands —like troughs on legs—that held the four big storage batteries.

The left antler snapped off at the base. Blood erupted from the flesh around it, streamed down to join with the blood that leaked from the animal's injured left eye.

The battery stands rocked wildly back and forth. A nail screeched as it was forced out of the wood. But the stands did not collapse.

The buck was dying. Blood poured from half a dozen cuts, but it was the eye injury that was serious.

Sensing the nearness of death, the animal panicked and tried to regain control of itself, tried to run. But the alien held its mind as tightly as a miser's fist might grip an extremely valuable gold coin.

The buck charged the battery stands again.

A battery fell to the ground. A cap popped from it. Acid gurgled across the barn floor.

151

Once again the buck threw himself into the stands, and once again dislodged a battery. But this time he also tore loose a live cable. Bam! Sparks exploded. Something went fitzzz! As the twisted end of the cable fell into the battery acid, the deer danced up onto its hind legs, twirled around in a full circle, at the mercy of the burst of current. But then the current was drained away, the generator finished at last, and the proud animal collapsed with an awful crash. Dead.

19.

Toby and I were halfway down the cellar steps, on our way to see about using the tarp for a sled, when the lights went off. Surprised, I grabbed hold of the railing to keep from falling in the darkness. "Something's happened to the generator."

Behind me Toby said, "You think those guys busted it up, Dad? Those guys from space?"

My first thought had been that the fuel supply was depleted or that the equipment had malfunctioned. But when Toby asked that question, I knew that those yellow-eyed bastards had gotten to the machinery and had ruined it. I remembered the dead bull and the battered generator on the Johnson farm, and I knew I could rule out the idea of a natural failure of the equipment.

(I should have foreseen all of that! For god's sake, there was that bull at the Johnson farm. How could I overlook the possibility? But I'd been so weary, propped up by hot showers and shots of whiskey and bowls of vegetable soup and hope, too weary to think clearly. Yet. . . Even if I had realized the danger, what could I have done about it? Come on, Hanlon, quit the breast beating. It's useless. I couldn't have stood guard in the barn all night, for they could have gotten to me too easily.)

"Dad?"

"You all right, son?"

"Sure. You okay?"

"Fine."

The darkness was absolute. I closed my eyes, squeezed them tight shut, opened them: still nothing.

"What next?" Toby said.

"We've got to get upstairs right away." As I heard him getting turned around on the steps above me, I said, "Be careful you don't trip and fall in the dark."

Connie was in the kitchen. "Don?"

"I'm here."

"I can't see you."

"I can't see you either."

"Where's Toby?"

"I'm okay, Mom."

I was feeling around with my hands, like a blind man.

Connie said, "Did *they* do it?"

"I'm afraid so."

"What's going to happen?"

"I don't know. Where are the guns?"

"The rifle's on a chair," she said. "The pistol's still on the table unless you have it."

"I don't."

"I've got the shotgun," she said.

"Here's the rifle," Toby said.

I stumbled toward him. "Don't touch that!"

"I just have my hand on the butt," he said. "I won't pick it up, Dad."

I found the table and then the pistol and then Toby. I picked up the loaded rifle.

"I'll find some candles," Connie said.

I said, "Maybe we should wait for them in the dark."

"I can't," she said. "I can't see anything, not anything at all—and I keep thinking they're already in the house, already in this room. I *have* to have light."

For an instant I expected to be touched by an inhuman hand—and then I realized that if the aliens were here with us in the kitchen, we would see their yellow eyes even in this pitch blackness. I said as much.

"I still have to have light," Connie said.

She fumbled through several drawers, found the matches, and struck up a flame.

She lit a candle.

Then two more.

We *were* alone.

For the moment.

20.

Outside:

With its mission accomplished, the lone alien walked away from the barn in which the dead buck (symbol of something) lay in a bloody heap. The creature's spindly but terribly strong legs poked deep into the snow and thrust forward, unhindered by the drifts. The thing joined its five companions where they stood just thirty yards from the back of the farmhouse.

Seemingly oblivious of the vicious wind and the blinding snow and the cutting sub-zero cold, the six yellow-eyed creatures lined up in a row. They looked quite like soldiers facing their enemy's position and readying their well planned assault.

Which, in fact, is precisely what they were and what they were doing.

(Throughout our ordeal—from the earliest moment of it, from the very minute that Toby found those strange tracks in the snow, from the instant I laid eyes on them—I had understood the symbology —both natural and psychological—that was operating in this affair. I had seen the parallels between these events in northern Maine and certain things I had endured in Southeast Asia. Perhaps I haven't commented in enough detail on this aspect of the matter; perhaps I haven't made the war analogy as obvious to you as it was to me, the war analogy and the Asian analogy. It is even possible that I played down my observations because I thought that, by reading such complex and fundamentally crazy meanings into these events, I was stretching a point, belaboring a theory—or maybe even, well, maybe I thought that such observations, when committed to type, might be construed as evidence of some renewed madness in me. Whatever. But, first of all, I am quite sane. My mind is as clear as glacial ice. And as dead as glacial ice—or about to be, as I write this. How long until I die? Each word I type is one less minute of life left to me. But what I want to say is that I *did* understand the frame of reference, did see the symbology which a madhouse universe had thrust upon me, giggling as it rushed past. Oh, I surely saw it all, yes. Oh, yes. I am not a stupid man, you know, and in fact I was valedictorian of my graduating class at Penn State, before the war, like everything else that I can think of in my life, before the war, before the stinking war. . . And yet. . . Somehow I overlooked the most obvious and important link between these science fictional events and the war in Vietnam. How could I have missed it? I've read all about Lieutenant Calley. I've read about My Lai and the massacres. Culture shock. The lack of social interaction. Man's inability to understand his fellow man, especially when skin color, politics, religion, and history separate them. I knew all about that: I was educated: I was a liberal. And yet I missed the point of all I've thus far told to you. It was like the war! It was Vietnam. It was, there in Maine, Vietnam all over again, the same pain, the same misunderstandings, the same mistakes, dammit!)

The yellow eyes glowed.

The aliens watched the house.

Were they frightened, so far away from home? Or were they, like arrogant American soldiers, sure of their right to dominate and destroy?

When ten minutes had passed, the creatures moved ten yards closer to the sun porch.

Then stopped.

And watched.

And waited.

And made ready.

21.

Inside:

In spite of the eighteen-inch-thick stone walls and the solid Revolutionary War construction which had been augmented by Twentieth Century fiberglas insulation, the farmhouse cooled rapidly once the heating system was knocked out of operation. There were six big fireplaces in the house, and the heat was sucked up and out of all of them while winter air rushed down the flues. Cold air rolled off all of the windows. Fifteen minutes after the lights went out, the air was decidedly chilly. Five minutes after that, the house was downright cold.

We dressed in woolen scarves, caps, gloves, and coats as soon as we realized that we should capture our body heat and hold on to as much of it as possible, before the house was like a refrigerator.

"Maybe we should build a fire," Connie said.

"Good idea."

"I'll help," Toby said.

"You stay with your mother." I shoved cordwood into the mammoth living room fireplace and packed starter material—wood shavings, paper, and sawdust—beneath the logs. I was about to light the paper when I had a sudden revelation. "My God!"

Connie whirled away from the windows, raising

159

the rifle that she held in both hands. The barrel gleamed in the candlelight. "What's the matter?"

"I just realized why these bastards knocked out our electric power," I said.

"Why, Dad?"

"Our oil furnace. It's sparked by an electric wick."

Connie said, "So?"

I was still thinking furiously. "And I think I know why they had to use a bull to destroy Ed's generator."

"Don, *tell* us."

I looked up and grinned. "They can't tolerate warmth."

"Warmth?"

"Fire, heat, warm air," I said excitedly. "These creatures must come from an extremely cold planet. They can't live in a room that's warm enough to be comfortable for humans. Maybe they like sub-zero weather like this. Maybe the temperature has to be below—oh, say freezing, before they can even tolerate a place. They had to send that bull in to wreck Ed's generator, because the tool shed on the Johnson farm was heated."

"We shouldn't have turned the heaters off in the barn," she said. "We gave them their chance."

"No," I said. "They'd have found some animal to use, just like the bull."

(Later, when I found the dead buck, I realized that they had used an animal even though there had been no heat in the barn for many hours. However, when they had stolen the horses from us, the barn *had* been heated. And when they'd planned their attack on us, they could not have known I'd let the barn cool off.")

"And now when it gets cold enough in here," Connie said, "they'll come after us."

We stared at each other for a long moment.

She said, "Better get that fire going."

I lit the paper, sawdust, and shavings.

"Can we keep them out with fire?" Toby asked.

"I don't know," I said "But we can darn sure try."

22.

Outside:

The six aliens split up into two groups of three each. One group moved off to the east and disappeared around the corner of the farmhouse. The others stayed where they were for another five minutes. Then they moved quickly toward the house.

The time had come.

23.

The crumpled paper flared up at once and ignited, in turn, the sawdust. In a few seconds the wood shavings began to catch, and then the dry bark of the cord wood smouldered and sparked. Gently fanning the growing flames, I smiled when the first vague trace of heat wafted out of the fireplace and across my face—

—and then the brief illusion of security and safety vanished as a pane of window glass shattered behind me, on the far side of the room.

Toby shouted.

Connie screamed.

Grabbing the shotgun off the flagstone hearth beside me, I rose, turned, and gasped involuntarily.

For the first time, by the light of the three candles, one of the aliens stood totally revealed. It was an insectlike being, and it was trying to smash its way through one of the three windows that opened onto the front porch. It looked somewhat like a praying mantis and a bit like a grasshopper—but it was really not like either of them. In size, of course, it was like no insect that the earth had ever known: seven feet tall at the head, sloping back for perhaps six or eight feet, with a thick body section, two forelegs as big around as my arms, and six other legs as thick as broomsticks and with three joints each. The thing's head was a yard long and two-foot wide, with those saucer-sized amber eyes, a rippled horny ridge running from between the eyes to the tip of the pointed snout, and saw-edged mandibles that seemed to work constantly as if chewing a tasty morsel. Snow clung to the creature as it struggled through the broken window; and paper-thin pieces of ice dropped from its shiny brown-black carapace. It tore out the window struts which separated the window panes and which barred its progress; although it appeared to be quite delicate, it was a fiercely strong creature.

A window shattered in another corner of the room, toward the rear of the house.

"Don!"

I turned in that direction.

A second alien was trying to get into the living room from the back lawn. Two heavy, hair-prickled, snow-dusted legs came through the window, chitinous legs as hard as metal, and scrabbled for a foothold.

I glanced at the fire. It was building slowly, but it was not throwing off enough heat to compensate for the cold air pouring in at the violated windows.

Glass exploded behind me again.

The second of the three big porch windows had been knocked in, and a third alien was gradually thrusting through the oversized frame.

The first alien to attack was almost inside now. Its large forelegs were firmly planted on the carpet; and only four of the other six legs were still out on the porch. Its enormous head swiveled from Connie to Toby to me to Connie. . .

I used both barrels of the shotgun on it, blew it backwards. Two of the smaller legs were torn off, and they clattered against the wall. The creature made a curious, keening noise and started toward me once more. By that time I had slipped two shells from my coat pocket and had reloaded. I used both shots on it, and it seemed to dissolve, tumbling through the window and onto the porch in a dozen pieces.

I jammed more shells into the chambers.

I felt mental fingers reaching for me, pressing against my skull, slipping inside of me. I fought back with all of my will—fought against not only the control it sought but against the mindless, biological fear it produced. That fear could incapacitate me; it had paralyzed me before. And if I were driven half-mad with fear now, there would be no hope for us.

Bones. . .

Connie used the rifle. It made a sharp, ear-splitting sound in the confines of the room.

I looked back and saw that the insect on her side of the room was three-quarters of the way inside and had not been stopped by the rifle fire.

Glass crashed.

A fourth alien was trying to come in from the third porch window. But that was of little consequence, for the creature at the second window was already inside and coming for me, its head swiveling, its amber eyes brighter than I have ever seen them, the big mandibles clacking noisily.

I raised the shotgun and pulled the first trigger without knowing if the thing was in my line of fire.

The alien halted, but it was not dead. It seemed stunned for an instant, but then it started forward once more.

I moved in close and discharged the second shot into its head, straight into the eyes.

Thankfully, it shuddered and toppled.

I groped for more shells, fed them into the gun, slammed the breach shut, and blasted the third alien out of the window and back onto the front porch.

The room was full of thunder. My ears ached.

Connie's rifle had been cracking repeatedly while I tended to the attackers on my side of the room, but she still had not been able to destroy the fourth alien. It seemed able to absorb the rifle bullets without damage—which meant that the shotgun was effective only because it packed considerably more wallop and spread it granulated charge over a broader area. As I reloaded my weapon, Connie dropped the rifle and ran to the fireplace, poked in the burning wood, and found a fairly long, slender piece of wood that was burning only at one end. She picked this up, turned, and ran back toward the beast.

"Connie, no!"

The thing was halfway across the room when she came upon it, and it backtracked the instant it saw the flames. Its mandibles made a snicking noise. Suddenly one of the three slender legs on its right side reached up to a bandolier slung across its back; fingerlike claws grasped a tubular device clipped to the bandolier.

"Connie, it's reaching for a weapon!"

She threw the burning branch.

When the flames touched it, the alien shrieked, an ungodly sound that made me shiver. It stumbled backwards, eight legs akimbo, and fell heavily to the floor. It burnt like a gasoline-soaked torch. It rolled and heaved and kicked, trying to get to the window. The insufferable stench—ammonia, carbon, decay— was so intense that it made me feel ill.

I emptied my shotgun into the thing in order to

put it out of its misery—then whirled around to see if any new beasts had come through the porch windows.

None had.

Everything was still, quiet.

Deafeningly quiet.

"Is it over?" Connie asked.

"Not that easily."

"There are more?"

"I'd bet on it."

"We can't hold out forever."

"We've done—"

We were both overcome with the same realization at the same instant, but she said it first: *"My God, where's Toby?"*

"He was here—"

"He isn't now!"

I ran out into the kitchen.

He wasn't there.

I heard her in the living room, shouting up the stairs.

The sun porch door was open. I hurried to it.

She rushed into the kitchen behind me.

I glanced back at her.

"Don, he doesn't answer me."

I went out onto the sun porch and found that the outer door was standing open. Snow was sweeping inside on the wind—and the snow just beyond the door was marked by a child's footprints and the eight-holed tracks I knew all too well.

Death is real.

Death is final.

"They've got him," she said.

The world is a madhouse.

"Their attack was only meant to distract us," she

said dazedly. "While we were distracted, they took control of Toby's mind and marched him right out of the house."

I turned and went back into the kitchen.

She came after me. "But four of them died! Would they sacrifice four of their own to get one of us?"

Real, final, real, final. . .

"Looks that way," I said, opening the box of shotgun shells that stood on the kitchen table. I began to fill my pockets.

She moaned softly.

"We've got to move fast," I told her. "Get your rifle and the box of ammunition. Hurry."

"We're going after them?"

"What else?"

She hesitated.

"Connie, hurry! We've got to catch the bastards before they. . . We've got to get Toby back from them!"

Leadenly: "What if he's already—dead?"

"And what if he isn't?"

"Oh, God!"

"Exactly."

She ran to get the rifle.

SATURDAY

The End

24.

It was an eerie pursuit upon which we engaged in that stark winter night: down the open hillside where the trail was only very slightly softened by the wind and the falling snow (which meant that they could not be far ahead of us, else their tracks would have been erased entirely), then along the perimeter of the trees for more than a hundred yards, and finally into the primeval northern forest. Under the pines, in the bleak wilderness, our flashlights were of more use to us than they had been out on the open land, for the snow did not blow and sheet before us, cutting our range of vision; and the yellow beams opened the night for twelve or fourteen feet ahead, like a scalpel slicing through skin. Connie went first along the narrow woodland trails, for I felt that if we were to be attacked, the enemy would surely try to surprise us from behind. After all, the flashlight revealed the way ahead and protected us from stumbling blindly into alien arms; therefore, the beasts might circle around us. She carried the rifle, and I carried the shotgun. Occasionally, spooked by the weird shadows caused by the dancing flashlight beams, one of us would bring up a gun and whirl and nearly open fire. And as we walked we kept glancing behind us: I did it to see if we were still alone, and Connie did it to see if the footsteps she heard behind her were still mine.

"We've come so far," she said at one point. "Why would they bring him so far?"

"I don't know."

But then a short while later I *did* know. Twenty minutes after we entered the forest, I realized that we were heading in the general direction from which that brilliant purple light had flashed at me two days ago, just after I had come out of the woods from finding Blueberry's skeleton. The light must have been some manifestation of their space craft: it marked the spot of their landing, their invasion base. And now they were taking Toby to their space ship . . .

For what?

Examination?

Tests?

Dissection?

Were they taking him as a specimen, taking him away into the stars?

We picked up our pace, walked as fast as we could manage, with less regard than before to the possibility of a surprise attack. Time was running out—fast.

I sensed that we were closing on them, that they might be no more than a few hundred yards along the trail. Once, I thought that mental fingers pressed lightly, so very lightly, against my skull, but I could not be certain. Nothing tried to force its way into me; but I *knew* that it was there and waiting.

We followed the trail up a hillock, down into a shallow ravine, around an outcropping of limestone.

And the ship lay before us.

Connie stopped.

I moved beside her and put one hand on her shoulder.

The ship stood in a clearing. It was a sphere at least one hundred and fifty feet in diameter, absolutely enormous, stunning. It towered over us, as high as a fourteen- or fifteen-story office building. There were no windows or doors or hatches, no marks of any kind upon it. The perfectly seamless pearl gray material from which it was made gave off a cold, cold light.

There was no noise at all. We could not even hear the wind moaning above us. And although we were in the open once more, well beyond the shelter of the trees, the wind did not touch us, and the snow did not fall here. Apparently, the sphere was enveloped in a subtle but effective shield, one which did not exclude its crew members or us, but which protected the vessel from earth's weather.

I felt like a savage as I stared up at the vast sphere, like a savage peering up through the jungle and catching his first glimpse of a passing jet airliner.

"Toby's in there," Connie said.

I didn't want to think about that.

"What are we going to do, Don?"

"Get him out."

"How?"

Before I could answer, I was struck from behind: hard. I was quite literally bowled from my feet, and I rolled end over end. I lost the shotgun; it went spinning off into the brush.

Connie cried out.

I heard a rifle boom.

Dazed, I got to my knees and looked up in time to see four aliens crowding in on her.

She fired again.

One of the beasts reached for the rifle with the claws at the end of its multi-jointed foreleg.

She backed up and fired.

In a rage one of the creatures rushed her, reared up on its four hindmost legs, and revealed a wicked yard-long stinger which had folded out of the forward part of its belly. The chitinous saber was bright green and dripped what could only be venom.

"Connie—"

The thing was on her in an instant, clutching her with its forelegs, plunging the stinger into her stomach. The razored tip of it came out of her back, streaming blood and yellow ichor.

There was no doubt that she was dead. The effect of the venom was really academic. The stab wound, gouged through vital organs, would have finished her in the blink of an eye.

I lost control. Madness swept over me. I began to scream and could not stop.

(It was not merely grief that had driven me over the edge. Oh God, I loved that woman, yes, loved her more than I loved myself. And what more can I say? What greater love could there be? When I lost her I knew that I had lost my reason for getting up in the morning. And yet there were other components of my madness. At the same time I suddenly realized that, just as in Vietnam, here were two cultures, two alien societies, clashing senselessly. Instead of trying to communicate, they had killed. And instead of trying to think of some way to reach them and make them understand, I had killed. Murder is always easier than judicious, reasoned action. Violence is not the resource of last resort for mankind (and for superior races such as these aliens) but it is the primary resource, the first reaction. And that is why there is no hope for a peaceful future, regardless of our scientific and technological advancements. We are flawed because the universe is flawed. The universe is a madhouse—and we are all madmen, whether humans or intelligent insects. And it was seeing this so clearly, as well as the grief, that sent me gibbering.)

I got to my feet, screaming and babbling unintelligibly, overwhelmed with hatred, self-hatred, and grief. I raised my fists and swung at the air and ran toward the nearest alien. I saw his stinger coming out of his belly, but I didn't care. In fact I wanted him to use it. I ran straight for him, screaming, screaming—

—and felt a pressure around my skull, then in my skull, then overwhelming me, pushing me down, taking full control, pushing me to the back of my own brain, pushing me into darkness . . .

25.

When I regained consciousness hours later I was in the farmhouse again. I was sitting behind the desk in the den. Through the window on my right I could see the crown of our hill and the barn bright red in the snow. Saturday must be well along, I thought, for the sky was light. The snow was falling, although not so fast and thick as it had been coming for days now.

I was not alone. One of the aliens was standing just outside the door of the den, watching me. Its mandibles clacked together, opened, clacked shut, opened . . . Another alien was in the room—and Toby stood at its side.

The boy's face was pale, his eyes blank. "Do you know where you are?" he asked me.

My mouth was dry. I nodded.

"Do you feel all right?"

I understood that I was not talking to Toby at all but to the alien beside him who was using Toby's brain and tongue and lips to communicate with me. I said, "I feel rotten."

"Physically or emotionally."

"Emotionally."

"That's all right," Toby-alien said.

"Maybe to you it is."

"We have found that we cannot control an adult mind or learn much from it. That is why I am not inside your head, speaking to you from within. You wouldn't permit it. You would be overwhelmed with fear and disgust. Therefore we will use your son to converse with you. Is that satisfactory?"

I said nothing.

"You are a writer," Toby-alien said.

I was surprised by this approach. I don't know what I had been expecting, but I certainly hadn't anticipated this. "No."

"You've written a book."

"One book. That doesn't make me a writer."

"Nevertheless, you can write. You can put these curious little symbols down on paper, order your ideas, convey your impressions and emotions to others of your kind."

Reluctantly, I said, "Yes."

"And perhaps to us."

"You killed my wife."

"That is beside the point."

"It *is* the point."

The alien's mandibles worked furiously, and its amber eyes regarded me with unknowable intent. Through Toby he said: "We cannot know what you are thinking by stepping into your mind. Your fear is so intense it blocks out your thoughts. But we want to know what you perceive of your existence and of the universe. We want to understand what evolutionary level you represent. Therefore, we wish you to put your thoughts into writing. We will read the writing through the eyes of your son and interpret your worthiness from the content thereof."

"My worthiness?" I said.

"You will write another book."

180

"About what?"

"You will write about us, about all that has happened here at Timberlake Farm during the last several days," Toby-alien said. "Then we will learn how you perceive us, and we will be able to put this affair in the proper perspective."

"No."

"No?"

"I won't write a book."

"You will write a book."

"You killed my wife."

"What does that matter?"

"Are you crazy?"

"We do not understand the concept of mental instability."

"Because you're all crazy and you have nothing sane to compare yourselves to," I said.

"You will write a book," Toby-alien said, and as he spoke he began to twitch. Spittle bubbled at the corners of his mouth.

"What are you doing to him?" I demanded.

"Nothing," the alien said through the boy. "But we find it difficult to use even a child. Such a strange species. He resists my thought control, and from time to time he throws fits much like those people you call epileptics."

"If I write the book, will you let Toby and me live? Will you go away from this world?"

"You will write a book."

"I need that promise."

"You will write a book."

As Toby began to twitch even more violently, I surrendered. "Okay. I'll write the book. I'll put it all down in print. Just don't torture the boy."

"I am not torturing him. This spasm is simply an

uncontrollable psychological reaction to my presence in his mind."

"You say you're using him as a tool for communication—but you're not speaking with his vocabulary."

"For the brief moments we were in your mind, your wife's mind, and the minds of the Johnsons, we absorbed all of your language. The boy is not a dictionary, just a translator and loud speaker."

"You killed the Johnsons."

"That does not matter."

"For God's sake!"

"Death does not matter."

"It's *all* that matters."

"Curious."

"I'll write the book," I said, slumping back in the chair.

"In three earth days."

"I can do it," I said. "I won't worry about style or grammar or punctuation. I'll just get the raw emotion down, the emotion and the fact."

"You will write a book."

"My typewriter is an electric model," I said. And then I realized that the lights were on. Not the heat, of course, for they couldn't tolerate it. But that would be turned on after they left.

"We have repaired the generator. Now we will leave you to your work."

They took Toby with them when they left. I watched them until they disappeared into the woods. Would I ever see him again?

On my way back to the den, I passed a photograph of Connie. It was in a silver frame on top of the piano. She played the piano well; I could almost hear her music. And the sight of her face was like a punch in the stomach. I doubled over and went to my knees and wept loudly.

Death is not mutable.

Death is not beatable.

Death is not cheatable.

Death is not a joke.

Death is real and final.

But the world is a madhouse.

Remember that. Don't take it seriously.

I don't know how long I remained on my knees, my head on the floor, weeping. A long time. Perhaps hours. When I finally got up, my chest ached and my throat was sore and my eyes burned.

But when I did get up I went into the den and rolled a sheet of paper into the typewriter. I would write the book. Somehow, I would hold myself together long enough to write the book. Connie was gone forever. But Toby was still alive. There was not much chance that they would let me have him or that they would let us live, but I had to hold onto even the frailest thread of hope. And so I kept telling myself: If you write the book, maybe you'll save yourself and Toby. And so I began to type.

26.

It's finished.

In three days I have written one hundred and eighty manuscript pages, and I am burnt out. I slept only one night out of three and took perhaps four or five one-hour naps. I have gotten through this ordeal with the aid of a fifth of Wild Turkey bourbon, a box of No-Doz caffeine tablets, and several bennies (prescribed for me in the days when I suffered bouts of lethargy and depression, just after I got out of the sanitarium). Bourbon, caffeine, and speed: that is not a good combination, not good at all. I stagger when I walk, and I can't think clearly any more.

But it's finished.

I will get up from this desk in a few minutes and go into the living room and sit down to wait for them. Somehow they will know that the book is written. What they expect to learn from it, I do not understand. It is obvious to me that our races are so terribly different—physiologically and psychologically—that no one book, no one man's explanations can ever bridge the gulf between us. They will study the text I have prepared, will be puzzled by it—and then, will they kill us?

It's finished.

Now let's finish the rest of it.

Come on, you bastards.

EPILOGUE

Some time during my lonely vigil I fell asleep on the couch. I didn't dream. But when I woke up, muttering to myself and wiping imaginary cobwebs from my face, there were two nightmares in the living room with me: two of the aliens stood before me with Toby between them.

The air was chilly. They had turned off the heating system long before they'd entered the house. I shivered uncontrollably.

I sat up and rubbed at my eyes and grimaced at the awful taste in my mouth. "It's finished," I told them.

As before they spoke to me through Toby. "We have read the manuscript."

"Already?"

"You have slept for more than twelve hours."

"Oh." I stood up, no longer intimidated by them. My face was within inches of one alien's clacking mandibles. "Have you learned anything from it?"

"Yes."

"What?"

"You would not understand."

"Try me."

"There are no concepts in your language—or mind."

"I see." But I didn't.

187

"Mr. Johnson and Mrs. Johnson cannot be restored. That was a mistake of ours. But he did kill one of us first," Toby-alien said.

Having a bit of trouble adjusting to the sudden change of topics, I said, "Well . . . What are you saying this for? Are you trying to absolve yourselves of guilt?"

"We do not comprehend the concept of guilt," Toby-alien said. "We merely wish, for whatever reasons, to set the record straight."

"Why are you on earth?"

"You could not understand."

"Why did you kill the horses—and strip them of flesh?"

"You have no concept of our motivations or purposes—and we barely understand the bizarre behavior you display."

I was getting nowhere fast, but the questions came compulsively. "Did you understand, at the start, that we were intelligent creatures?"

"We don't believe you are intelligent creatures," Toby-alien said as mandibles rattled noisily on both sides of him.

"What?"

"You do not conform in any way to our concept of intelligence. You are—barbaric, crude, disgusting. We believe that you are only extremely clever animals, able to feign activities and attitudes that would indicate the most basic periphereal intelligence."

"Then why are you bothering to try to communicate?"

Toby-alien said, "Because there is the slightest chance that we may be wrong. You may be intelligent, some exceedingly strange manifestation of the universal force of awareness."

188

Hope seeped back into me. "Then we will be allowed to live?"

"Yes," Toby-alien said. "We will leave this world within the hour. We have no desire to learn more of your culture, real or just contrived, whichever it may be."

"I think that's the wrong attitude."

Changing the subject again, Toby-alien said, "Your wife is upstairs, in the master bedroom, sedated."

My legs trembled. I thought I was going to collapse. "My wife is dead."

"She was dead."

"Then she still is."

"Why must that be so?"

"Death is final."

"This proves your race is not intelligent."

"Death is final, dammit!"

"It never is."

"I killed four of your people," I said. The corpses had been removed days ago; all that remained as evidence of the battle was the broken glass.

"We have removed their brains, which reside in impregnable pods beneath the carapace. The brains were put into newly cultured bodies. They live."

"And you built a new body for Connie?"

"That was not necessary. There are other methods."

"Tell me. I must know them."

"If you were an intelligent creature, you would already know them," Toby-alien said. "And since you are an unintelligent beast, the concept would do you no good. You would not understand it."

The aliens turned and stalked out of the room.

They were finished with me, and they never looked back.

Toby said, "Dad? What's going on here? I'm scared." His voice trembled.

"It's over," I assured him. I picked him up and hugged him. "There's nothing to be afraid of now."

"Where's Mom?"

"Let's go find her," I said, a lump rising in my throat.

I carried him upstairs.

She was sitting up in bed when we got there. She was as beautiful as ever. "Don?"

"I'm here."

"Toby?"

"Hi, Mom."

Death is not final.

But the universe is still a madhouse. There is meaning in it, yes, but random meaning, a lunatic's planning, the purpose of a spastic Planner.

And we are lunatics in this madhouse, but we have learned to live with it—a necessity, since there is no hope of being released from it. As Toby and I sat on the edge of the bed and the three of us hugged one another, the night was filled with our maniacal but undeniably happy laughter.

ROGER ELWOOD talks about

Laser Books

No. 1. Renegades of Time by R. F. Jones
Ray Jones can tell a story as well as any man. Read this and see what I mean.

No. 2. Herds by Stephen Goldin
Steve Goldin's ability to weave the alien world into the fabric of our contempory world is uncanny.

No. 3. Crash Landing On Iduna by Arthur Tofte
Written by an "old pro". As you'd expect, it's adventure as it should be written with an ending that will surprise!

No. 4. Gates Of The Universe by Robert Coulson and Gene DeWeese
This top flight writing team have come up with a winner. Several of their characterizations are really outstanding.

No. 5. Walls Within Walls by Arthur Tofte
This is Arthur's second novel in the series. It has beauty and grace and much human understanding. A rare combination in a S.F. adventure. I think you'll agree.

No. 6. Serving In Time by Gordon Eklund
Gordon is really establishing himself in the S.F. world. With this exciting tale, he gives us a lesson in history too.

No. 7. Seeklight by K.W. Jeter
As Barry Malzberg says in his introduction, "one of the three or four best first S.F. novels I have read."

No. 8. Caravan by Stephen Goldin
As I said about his first novel in our series, "His ability to weave the alien world into the fabric of our contempory world is uncanny."

MORE EXCITING TITLES ON NEXT PAGE!

No. 9. **Invasion** by Aaron Wolfe
This is the first novel Aaron Wolfe has ever written. As Barry Malzberg says of it, "It is simply one of the most remarkable first novels, in any field, that I have ever read."

No. 10. **Falling Toward Forever** by Gordon Eklund
This is Gordon's second offering in our series. It's straight S.F. adventure this time, with a deeply human thread, and it's very, very good.

No. 11. **Unto The Last Generation** by Juanita Coulson
Juanita is the wife of Robert Coulson, a co-author of Laser Book No. 4. I think you'll really enjoy her story and that you'll delight in the poetic mood she manages to convey.

No. 12. **The King of Eolim** by Raymond F. Jones
A deeply sensitive story about a family whose son is retarded by their society's standards. At the same time there's lots of excitement and adventure. It takes a Ray Jones to blend these two elements as masterfully as this story does it.

ORDER BOOKS WITH HANDY ORDER FORM BELOW!